Who Is There . . . ?

Christina heard someone moan.

She dropped the bucket. Water splashed onto the hallway floor. The moan came again, louder this time.

Is Emily sick? Heart pounding, Christina crept closer to Emily's door. She didn't want anything to do with Emily. But she couldn't ignore her. What if she hurt herself somehow?

Christina put her hand on the latch. I can't just pretend I didn't hear anything. I've got to find out what's going on!

"Don't go in there!" a voice behind her shrieked.

Christina spun around. Emily glared at her from the top of the stairs.

Christina heard the moan again.

If Emily is out here, who is that moaning in her room?

FEAR STREET SAGAS® #4
R.L. STINE

The Sign of Fear

A Parachute Press Book

AN ARCHWAY PAPERBACK
Published by POCKET BOOKS
New York London Toronto Sydney Tokyo Singapore

AN ARCHWAY PAPERBACK *Original*

An Archway Paperback published by
POCKET BOOKS, a division of Simon & Schuster Inc.
1230 Avenue of the Americas, New York, NY 10020

Copyright © 1996 by Parachute Press, Inc.

THE SIGN OF FEAR WRITTEN BY CAMERON DOKEY

ISBN: 0-671-00291-0

First Archway Paperback printing December 1996

10 9 8 7 6 5 4 3 2 1

FEAR STREET is a registered trademark of Parachute Press, Inc.

AN ARCHWAY PAPERBACK and colophon are registered trademarks of Simon & Schuster Inc.

Cover art by Lisa Falkenstern

Printed in the U.S.A.

IL 7+

Prologue

The New World
Western Pennsylvania Frontier, 1710

Matthew Fier laughed and laughed. He couldn't stop. He started laughing days ago—when he triumphed over his enemy William Goode.

But triumph came with a price. And Matthew Fier knew it. I am going to laugh myself into my grave, he thought.

Matthew's stomach muscles ached. His throat felt raw and sore. But he laughed on.

He spread a layer of mortar over the top row of bricks. Soon all the walls of his study would be brick from floor to ceiling. No windows. No doors. Nothing but strong bricks to keep them safe.

The Goodes will never be able to reach us, he thought. Not once I wall us in. They will never get their hands on the Fier amulet. They will never get their hands on the power of the Fiers.

Matthew placed another row of bricks in the wet mortar. He pushed himself to work faster. As he worked, he pictured the Fier amulet.

A shiny silver disk with a bird's claw on the front. The claw clutching bright blue stones. And on the back, the words the Fiers lived by: *Dominatio per malum.* Power through evil.

Matthew knew the history of the amulet. It had been passed down from father to son for hundreds and hundreds of years.

The amulet was old. So old he could hardly imagine it. Before the time of recorded history it belonged to a young Celtic spell-caster called Fieran.

The dark power of Fieran's amulet would never die—as long as one Fier still lived to claim it.

I will die soon, Matthew thought. He laughed as he set the last brick in place, completing the final wall. Yes, soon I will die. But someday another Fier will come. A Fier who will claim the amulet.

Matthew remembered another time when the amulet had to be protected. It had been lost and Matthew reclaimed it from a woman. What was her name?

Matthew felt dizzy. A buzzing sound filled his ears. Images from his past flashed through his mind.

Christina! he thought suddenly. Christina Davis! That was her name.

She had the amulet when I found it.

Matthew drew another breath.

This is the last I will ever take, he realized. He held it for a moment.

A red haze filled his vision.

Fire, he thought. There was a fire the night I

received the amulet from Christina. And a fire the night Fieran first beheld the amulet.

Christina . . . Fieran.

Fire . . . Fier.

The amulet. The amulet. The amulet.

Matthew wheezed as he released his final breath.

PART ONE

Betrayal

Chapter
1

The New World
Massachusetts Bay Colony,
1679

Christina Davis stared down into the open grave. Wide and black. It reminded her of a huge mouth.

Oh, Papa! Christina thought. I don't want to be alone. Why did you leave me? A strangled sob escaped her throat.

Hard, bony fingers dug into Christina's arm. "Shame me and you'll live to regret it," her aunt whispered in her ear. "Displaying so much emotion in public is improper. Control yourself, girl!"

Christina pressed her lips together. Don't cry, she told herself. Not in front of Aunt Jane. She concentrated on taking deep, slow breaths. Gradually, her aunt released her painful grip.

How could I have thought I was alone? Christina asked herself. She closed her eyes for an instant. I will never be alone. There will always be Aunt Jane.

Aunt Jane!

She hates me, Christina thought. Always criticizing. Calling me stupid and lazy. Slapping me when I make even a tiny mistake.

But never in front of Papa. No, in front of Christina's father Aunt Jane acted soft and loving. She waited until she had Christina alone to scream at her. Punish her.

Now she will always have me alone, Christina thought. Now I have no one to protect me.

The minister stepped forward and cleared his throat. "Brethren," he began in a deep, loud voice. "Let us pray."

Christina heard a soft rustle as the assembled townspeople clasped their hands before them. She bowed her head with the rest of the congregation. Her eyes focused on the hem of her dark mourning dress. On the square toes of her thick, black shoes.

Dear God in Heaven, she prayed silently. Welcome my father into your loving embrace. And help me find a way to escape.

Christina caught her breath. Yes, that was what she had to do. She had to escape. She had to run away from Aunt Jane.

With a firm "amen," the prayer ended. The townspeople lifted their heads. Four strong men moved forward. They began to lower Christina's father's coffin into the grave with stout ropes. The wood of the coffin groaned and creaked.

Scalding tears burned Christina's eyes. Oh, Papa, she thought. Things could have been so different. If only you hadn't gotten sick.

Her father's coffin hit the bottom of the grave with a thud. Through the haze of her tears, Christina saw the minister beckon to her. He pointed one bony finger at a pile of earth alongside the grave.

Christina's stomach clenched. She understood what the minister wanted. She had to throw the first handful of earth into her father's grave.

Christina could feel the eyes of the townspeople upon her. Her legs felt stiff as she moved forward. She bent down, and scooped up a handful of cold, clammy earth. A fat, purple worm wiggled between her fingers.

Christina could almost see the worms' dark bodies sliding in and out of her father's clean, white bones.

She couldn't stand the feel of the dirt on her fingers one more second. She flung it into the grave with all her strength. Then she backed away.

Aunt Jane strode forward. She didn't hesitate as Christina had. She scooped a handful of dirt up and hurled it into the grave with one powerful stroke. Then she moved back to Christina's side.

One by one, the townspeople approached Christina and her aunt and paid their respects. One by one, they threw handfuls of dirt into her father's grave.

Thunk. Thunk. Thunk.

Christina mumbled her thanks to the townspeople without listening to what they said. Her eyes locked on the dirt filling her father's grave.

Why does it have to be Papa we bury? she thought. Why couldn't it have been Aunt Jane?

At exactly that instant, the sun went out.

Christina gasped. She stared up into the sky. It boiled with dark shapes. The sound of hundreds of beating wings echoed off the hillsides.

Crows. The entire sky is filled with crows.

Christina opened her mouth to scream, but no sound came out. She wanted to run, but her legs wouldn't move.

A crow dove toward her. Its yellow beak opened wide. It grabbed a thick lock of Christina's hair and yanked it out of her head. She felt warm blood flow down the side of her head and trickle into her ear.

The minister uttered a high, shrill scream. Christina jerked her head toward him—and saw a crow tear a piece of flesh from his cheek.

A woman shoved her way past Christina, dragging her two sobbing children behind her. One of the children fell to the ground. The crows surrounded it, jabbing and pecking. The woman tried to drive them off, screeching and flapping her cloak.

Christina ran to her aid. The crows slashed at her legs, ripping through her black dress and cutting into her flesh. She ignored the pain and pulled the child to his feet. "Run!" she urged.

She heard Aunt Jane begin to pray behind her. Christina turned to face her aunt—and saw a huge crow ready to attack.

Caw! Caw! Caw!

The crow hurled itself straight at Christina.

Christina bent down and frantically searched for a weapon. She grabbed a stone that fit perfectly in the palm of her hand. Then she straightened and hurled the stone as hard as she could.

Thunk! The stone hit the crow on the head. It fell to the ground with one last cry.

But another crow came right behind it. A crow with something shiny and silver grasped in its beak.

Christina scrambled for another rock. No time. The bird was too close. So close Christina could see the gleam of its black eyes.

Christina threw her hands over her head. Her fingers tangled on the silvery object the bird held in its beak. The bird flapped its wings wildly, trying to escape. She felt the hot, musty air hitting her face.

Caw! Caw! Caw! The bird tore free and wheeled in the air. Then it dove toward Christina again.

Christina stumbled backward. She felt the earth crumble beneath her feet. Felt herself begin to fall.

Fall into her father's open grave.

Chapter
2

A heavy weight pressed down on Christina. She struggled against it. But her arms and legs would not move. She was pinned in place. Her body completely useless.

She remembered falling. Falling and landing in a hole. No. Not a hole—her father's grave! *I've been buried alive!*

Christina's eyes popped open. She rested in her own bed, the covers tightly tucked around her.

Christina loosened the blankets and sat up. How did I get here? She had no memory of going home.

Perhaps I fainted when I fell. Some of our neighbors must have helped Aunt Jane bring me home.

Christina's tongue felt dry and swollen. She needed a cool drink of water. She swung her legs over the side of the bed. Pain shot through her body. I must be covered with bruises, she thought.

The floorboard outside Christina's door creaked. Aunt Jane checking up on me, Christina thought. She quickly stretched out and pulled the covers up to her chin. She did not want to speak with her aunt now. The day had been hard enough already.

Christina heard the door swing open and the whisper of skirts against the floor. She struggled to make her breathing slow and even. Leave, she thought. Go away and leave me alone.

"She still sleeps," Aunt Jane murmured. "That is good. If she is tired it will make things that much easier for us."

Who is she talking to? Christina wondered. Why did she bring someone into my room?

"You are certain you wish to do this?" a second person asked, the voice low and harsh. But a woman's voice, Christina felt sure.

"Of course I'm certain," Aunt Jane snapped. "I would not have asked you to come here otherwise, now would I?"

The women moved closer. Christina could feel their hot breath on her face. Stay calm, she told herself. Don't move. Don't move.

What is she planning? Christina thought. What is Aunt Jane going to do to me?

"We should do it tonight," the woman murmured. Aunt Jane grunted in agreement.

"And her absence?" the woman asked. "How will you explain that?"

My absence? Is she sending me away? Christina thought. Almost any place would be better than here with her aunt.

"'Tis none of your concern," Aunt Jane answered. She sounded annoyed. "Leave it to me."

"It is my concern," the woman insisted, her voice growing louder. "I have a right to know. You will put me in danger if you handle it badly."

"You saw her at the graveside today," Aunt Jane

said impatiently. She stepped away from the bed. "It's plain her grief for her father has upset the balance of her mind. She might do anything in this state. She might even wander off . . . and become lost in the woods around the town. An unprotected girl, alone, would meet all sorts of dangers."

"Dangers in the woods," the woman echoed. "Ah, yes, I see."

"Naturally, I would be terribly distraught should any harm come to my niece," Aunt Jane continued.

Evil, Christina thought. She is pure evil.

The other woman laughed. A harsh, ugly sound. "I'm certain the entire town will join me in extending my sympathy for your difficult situation."

"A kind thought. I thank you." Christina could almost hear her aunt smiling. "We're agreed, then?"

"Oh, aye," the woman answered. "We're agreed."

Christina heard the soft *clink* of coins changing hands. Then the sound of footsteps moving toward the door.

"I'll return tonight," the woman said, as the bedroom door creaked open.

"At midnight," Aunt Jane suggested. "No one else will be awake."

"Very well, at midnight, then." The bedroom door shut on the rest of their conversation.

Christina remained motionless. Her heart pounding so hard she feared it would choke her.

The moment she heard the large, heavy front door close, she bolted upright.

Aunt Jane is planning to kill me!

Chapter
3

Christina threw back the covers and scrambled out of bed. She had to escape. She had to run away. *Now!*

If I'm here when Aunt Jane returns, I'm trapped, Christina thought. She won't let me out of her sight.

Christina tiptoed over to her bedroom window. The scrubbed wood floor felt icy against her bare feet. She carefully parted the checkered curtains—just an inch—and peered out.

She saw her aunt helping a woman into a wagon in the far corner of the yard. Christina couldn't make out the woman's face.

Go! Go now! a voice inside Christina urged. Aunt Jane could come back in the house at any moment.

She darted over to the chest and grabbed her long cloak. Then she realized she wore only a nightgown.

I don't have time! she thought. Aunt Jane will be back before I am ready! Christina's heart began to hammer in her chest. She felt light-headed, her ears ringing.

Stop it, she ordered herself. This is no time to fall apart. She reached for the lacings of her nightgown. Her fingers slipped and fumbled. Something clattered to the floor.

What was that? Christina thought. She noticed a silver pendant next to her feet. Where did that come from?

Even in the dim light of her bedroom it glimmered. It seemed to glow with a strange light of its own. Fascinated, Christina picked it up. The silver disc felt warm. Comforting.

She ran her fingers over the silver bird's claw on the front. Over the six clear blue stones clutched in the claw.

A memory stirred in Christina's mind. A memory of an enormous black bird flying down at her. Something silver clutched in its beak. She remembered striking out at the bird—and her fingers becoming tangled in a thin chain.

That's how I got it. It's beautiful, she thought. So beautiful. And it's mine.

Christina lifted the chain over her head and slid on the silver pendant. Then she blinked several times. Why am I just standing here?

Within moments, she dressed in her sober black mourning dress, thick stockings and heavy, square-toed shoes. She hesitated over her white cap and apron.

I'd better leave them off, she thought. The white color might attract attention. She knew people considered it scandalous to go out bareheaded. But she could use the hood of her dark cloak.

Ready, she thought. She took a quick look around

her bedroom. This is the last time I will ever be here, she thought. The last time I will ever call this place my home.

"Good-bye, Papa," Christina whispered. "I'm sorry I won't be able to visit your grave. But I know you'll understand what I'm doing. Why I can never come back here."

Choking back her tears, Christina hurried to the door and pulled it open.

Creak.

Did Aunt Jane hear that? Is she back in the house? Christina held her breath. But the hall remained empty. The house silent.

Christina dashed down the hallway. Once she made it out the back door, Aunt Jane would never catch her.

Bang! The front door opened.

Oh, no! Christina thought. Now she couldn't make her way to the back door without Aunt Jane spotting her.

Christina crept back down the hallway. Placing each foot carefully so she wouldn't make the smallest sound.

Tap.

One of Christina's heels hit the floorboards.

She hesitated. Not a word from her aunt.

Almost there, she thought. Almost to my room.

Christina pulled in a deep breath and took another step.

"Christina Davis! What are you doing out of bed?" her aunt shrieked.

Christina raced into her room and slammed the door behind her. Do something! she ordered herself. Do something!

Christina picked up her dressing-table chair. Can I use it to block the door?

Aunt Jane's heavy footsteps thundered down the hall.

In another moment, she'll be here!

Christina whirled around. She flung the chair through her bedroom window with all her strength. Glass shattered. Jagged shards flew through the air.

Aunt Jane uttered a high, shrill scream of outrage.

Christina threw herself across the windowsill. Jagged glass bit into her arms as she dragged herself forward. Thank goodness her bedroom was on the first floor.

She could see Aunt Jane's vegetable garden beneath her. One more shove and I should make it. One more shove and I'll be free.

She hurled herself forward with all her might.

Then Christina's body jerked to a stop. Her aunt's cold, bony fingers wrapped around her ankle.

Chapter
4

Christina screamed. She slammed her free leg backward. Aiming for her aunt.

Missed.

Aunt Jane yanked Christina back across the windowsill. Shards of glass stabbed into her stomach.

"No!" Christina shouted. She kicked and squirmed, fighting to free herself. "I won't let you! *No!*"

"You can't stop me," Aunt Jane panted. "You're not strong enough."

"I'm stronger than you think I am," Christina cried. She grabbed the windowsill with both hands, pulling herself forward. She felt warm blood flowing from both palms. But she didn't care. She had to escape.

Aunt Jane grabbed Christina's calf with her free hand. She grunted with exertion. Using all her strength to pull Christina back inside.

Christina could feel her leg growing numb. She dug her fingernails into the wood of the window frame.

"Give up!" Aunt Jane demanded.

Christina felt her fingers slipping. One of her fingernails tore free. Pain shot up her arm.

I can't do this! Christina thought. She is too strong. So much stronger than I am. She let her body go limp.

Aunt Jane struggled to pull Christina's dead weight back into the house.

I have one chance left, Christina thought. One chance.

Slowly she bent her free leg up as far as she could.

Now I have to distract her. Christina did the last thing her aunt would expect. She lifted her head and looked back at Aunt Jane. Defiantly.

Aunt Jane's eyes blazed with fury. Her face turning brick red. "Wretched creature," she gasped. "Spiteful, *hateful* girl. You have been nothing but trouble since the day you were born. But you won't trouble me much longer now!"

Christina shoved her bent leg straight back. Her heavy shoe caught Aunt Jane squarely in the throat.

With a strangled cry, Aunt Jane collapsed on the floor.

Christina plunged forward. She landed headfirst in her aunt's vegetable garden. Dirt clogged her mouth. She sat up, gagging and choking.

She shoved herself to her feet and ran with all the strength she possessed. I did it! I'm free!

She ran into the woods until she could run no longer. Until her breath rasped in her throat and her legs felt as heavy as cannonballs.

Don't stop. Keep going, Christina told herself.

Stumbling with weariness, she forced herself to continue on.

Sweat rolled down her face, stinging her eyes. Her long skirt snagged on a bush, slowing her down.

Traveling on the road itself would have been easier. And faster. But it was too dangerous. Anyone could see her. Anyone.

Aunt Jane will not come after me. Will not, will not, will not. Christina chanted to herself with the rhythm of her footfalls. She wants me dead. Dead, dead, dead. She will not come after me.

Sharp pain jabbed into Christina's side. It hurt each time she tried to take a deep breath. I have to slow down for a little while, she thought. I have to rest.

The shadows in the woods grew thick and heavy all around her. The memory of Aunt Jane's face flashed through Christina's mind. Eyes filled with fury. Lips twisted in disgust.

She hates me, Christina thought. I knew she disliked me. I knew she resented opening her home to me. But I never realized she hated me. And wanted me dead.

Snap.

What was that? It sounded like someone stepping on a twig. Christina stopped and listened. She heard a faint rustling sound. It could be the wind in the trees, she decided. Or a small animal.

She felt cold suddenly. Her sweaty clothes chilly against her skin. She rubbed her arms, trying to get warm. Then she continued making her way through the woods.

Snap.

There it is again. Is someone following me? Christina turned and peered into the shadows behind her.

Nothing.

Your imagination is running away with you, Christina scolded herself. She turned back around and began to walk. Then she began to trot.

Snap! Snap! Snap!

Christina didn't stop to look behind her. She forced herself to pick up her pace. She ran through the forest. Tree branches slapping at her face.

Her toe caught on a root—and she flew into the air. She landed hard. Pain speared through her right foot.

Christina sat up and cradled her foot in her hand. She could feel her ankle swelling already.

SNAP!

I can't run. What am I going to do?

The bush nearest Christina rustled—and a fawn burst out. It bounded past, leaving Christina all alone.

A deer, Christina thought. A little deer almost scared me to death. She started to push herself to her feet. A jolt of pain shot through her ankle.

Christina collapsed back on the ground. She wished she could curl up and go to sleep. Forget about Aunt Jane. Forget about her father's funeral. Forget about the pain in her ankle. Forget about everything.

Maybe some sprite or elf will find me and care for me, she thought. Christina loved stories of these magical creatures when she was a little girl.

Christina shook her head. No time for daydreaming, she told herself. You are still in danger. You have to get farther away from Aunt Jane.

Besides, the air smells like rain. It is going to storm tonight. You need to find some kind of shelter. She struggled to her feet, wincing when she put pressure on her ankle.

At least it's not broken, Christina thought. She

limped through the forest, watching the uneven ground. She didn't want to fall again.

It grew harder and harder to see the forest floor. The sun is almost set, she realized. It will be dark soon. A lump formed in Christina's throat. What am I going to do? she thought.

If Papa were here, what would he advise? she asked herself.

Something practical, Christina thought. Papa was that kind of man. She could almost hear her father's voice:

"It is too dark and dangerous to keep going in the forest, Christina, my sweet girl."

I'm going to have to walk along the road, Christina thought. The last rays of the sun were dying as she reached the roadway. She noticed the thick, black clouds gathering. I was right, she thought. It's going to pour.

The road led up a hill. Christina gritted her teeth and began to climb.

When she reached the top, she had to stop and rest. Her ankle throbbed. Her arms and legs felt so heavy. She didn't know how much farther she could go.

Christina stared down at the tiny valley spread out before her. A few lights burned through the darkness, clear and strong. *Lights.* It's a farm, she realized.

That meant people—and a place to stay. She could spend the night in a warm, safe place. She felt sure the people who owned the farm would allow her to sleep in their barn.

Christina spotted a flash of lightning in the distance. A roll of thunder sounded.

Better hurry, she thought. She started down. Big raindrops began to fall. Icy water quickly soaked her hair. Her drenched skirts felt thick and heavy around her legs.

A burst of thunder exploded.

Christina began to run. Her ankle gave way. She slammed to the ground.

She tried to scramble to her feet. But she slipped on the muddy ground.

A shrill scream rang out behind her.

Chapter
5

The Old World
Britain, A.D. 50

Fieran screamed until his throat felt raw. *"Victory! Vic-tor-y!"*

I killed the Roman leader, he thought. Victory is ours! Fieran could feel the hot blood rushing through his veins. His heart pounded hard and fast.

He held the head of the Roman leader high in the air. The Celtic soldiers surrounding Fieran cheered and whistled.

All except Conn, Fieran noticed. Conn simply stared at Fieran with his cold blue eyes.

He has always hated me, Fieran thought. Ever since we were children. He is never satisfied until he has something I do not. Sometimes Fieran wondered if Conn would pursue Brianna if he did not know that Fieran loved her.

Conn should be happy I killed the Roman leader, Fieran thought. It means we are sure to win this battle. Instead he sulks because the others cheer for me.

Fieran stared up at the Roman leader's head. The ragged muscles of its neck dripped blood.

The head of my enemy brings me power, Fieran thought. More power than Conn will ever have. I now have the power to do anything. Anything! I can marry Brianna. I can become the leader of my people. I can become chief.

The battle is not yet over, Fieran reminded himself. First, we must drive the Roman invaders from our land—and make certain that not one comes back.

"Celts! To me!" Fieran cried out. He gave the signal for the final charge.

With a mighty roar, the Celts rushed forward. They met the soldiers of the Roman line head-to-head.

The Romans appeared desperate. Good, Fieran thought. You laughed at us. When we made our first charge, you laughed because you thought we were barbarians. Easy to kill.

You are not laughing any longer.

Fieran made his charge. He waved the Roman head above him like a flag of victory.

Behind him, he heard a savage battle cry. One of the Romans must have broken through our line! Fieran thought. They want the head back.

No one will take it from me! No one! Fieran spun to face the attacking soldier, bringing his long sword up to protect his chest. "I am ready for you!" he cried.

"And I am ready for you, Fieran."

What? Fieran lowered his sword slightly.

Conn stood before him.

"I warn you, Conn. Stay back. I do not want to kill you."

Conn smiled. "I am glad to hear you say that, Fieran. Because you are not going to kill me. *I* am going to kill *you!*"

Conn charged, his sword aimed at Fieran's chest.

Chapter
6

Fieran leapt back. He slammed his sword down on Conn's.

Metal shrieked against metal.

Fieran and Conn locked eyes. The cords in Conn's neck stood out as he struggled to force Fieran's sword down.

Conn stood taller than Fieran and weighed more. Fieran had to use all his strength to keep Conn's sword from slamming down on him. His sword arm began to tremble.

Fieran dug his feet into the ground. He didn't let Conn's sword move an inch. But he couldn't push it back.

"You hate to see me with such power, don't you Conn?" Fieran demanded. "Accept it. From now on I will always be stronger. From now on I will always win."

"You are weak." Conn sneered. "You will never be

able to control the power of the head. You will never be able to use it for our people—as I can."

Fieran's arm shook. He hoped Conn could not see his sword jiggling. I have to do something now, he thought. In a contest of pure strength, Conn will win.

Now. Fieran jerked his sword down—away from Conn's. Conn's sword fell forward. Fieran circled his sword up and around. He crashed it down on Conn's before Conn had a chance to recover.

Conn's sword snapped in two.

Conn stumbled, and Fieran knocked him to the ground. He kicked the pieces of Conn's sword away. "I should kill you," Fieran told him. "You are a creature of evil and I should kill you now."

Conn's blue eyes remained icy. He did not appear frightened. He made no attempt to escape from Fieran.

The Celts need every warrior to battle the Romans, Fieran thought. If I kill Conn, I kill one of our best soldiers. Slowly he lowered his sword.

Nothing could come before the good of Fieran's people. Not even his hatred of Conn.

"Join the other soldiers," he ordered.

Conn slowly stood. "I would not have allowed you to live," he said. "I know what to do with power. You never will." He turned and sprinted toward the battle.

Fieran glanced around. No one appeared to have noticed his fight with Conn. All the men battled fiercely against the Romans. Good.

The Roman soldiers are retreating, he realized. The Celts chased after them. We won!

The danger is past, he thought. The soldiers don't need me any longer.

Fieran started for the woods that bordered on the battlefield. With the battle over, he realized his whole body ached with weariness. How good it would feel to be home!

As he walked, he thought back to the night his father told him about the cult of the head. It was the night before he died in battle.

"Taking an enemy's head is the greatest triumph a warrior can have," his father explained. "All a warrior's power is located there."

"But that doesn't make sense," the young Fieran protested. "A warrior's power must be in his arms. To throw his spear or stab with his sword."

Fieran remembered that his father smiled. "That is what I used to think," he said. "Until my father told me the secret."

Fieran's father knelt down on the ground beside his son's sleeping pallet. "So now I'm telling you, Fieran. A man's power is here, in his head." His father touched his finger to his own head and then to Fieran's.

"His head is where he dreams his dreams of conquest. His head is where he makes his battle plans. Take a man's head, and you take the best part of him. But beware the bargain you must make, Fieran."

Intrigued, Fieran stared up at his father. "What kind of bargain, Father?" he asked.

"Power always comes with a price," his father answered. "To gain power, you must give up something. Be careful you do not give too much."

I have given nothing, the grown-up Fieran thought. Wherever you are now, Father, I hope that you are proud of me.

Most of Fieran's people lived in a village on a nearby hilltop. From there they could see enemies approaching for miles around—a good, strong position for a village. But Fieran had never lived there.

Fieran didn't feel comfortable around the other

Celts. He was different from most of them. He was a spell-caster.

The spell-casters formed a special class among the Celtic people. They possessed great knowledge, and powerful magic.

Fieran did not have to fight today. The Celts did not require it of spell-casters. But he did not like to hide behind his book learning. He enjoyed meeting his enemy face-to-face.

Why does Conn have to be a spell-caster too? Fieran thought. If he wasn't I could avoid him. Fieran frowned as he crossed the tiny stream that flowed through the forest.

The water felt good on his tired feet. Fieran liked living in the forest. Woods were places of power for his people. The most sacred glade of all was not far from Fieran's own dwelling place.

Too bad Conn is my only neighbor, Fieran thought. None of the others made their home in the forest.

What am I going to do about him? Conn won't be happy until I'm dead. I know it.

Fieran reached his cave deep within the forest. He pushed aside the screen of vines that covered the mouth of the cave and stepped inside.

I will begin working on the head right away, he thought. Once I learn to control its power, I will never need to worry about Conn again. He will never be able to defeat me. And he will never be selected as the new chief.

Fieran cradled the head in both palms. The power locked inside would bring him everything he wanted. Everything.

Pain shot through his hands. Burning, sizzling pain. Fieran cried out. He dropped the head on the floor. The world exploded in a ball of flame. Surrounding Fieran in a solid wall of fire.

Chapter 7

Fieran's body jerked as the flames licked at it. He heard his hair snap and sizzle. Felt his skin curl away from his bones.

Fire blazed in every direction. No way to escape.

Fieran's eyeballs felt like hot coals. His tongue felt dry and gritty.

He collapsed onto his knees. Each breath burned his lungs.

Fieran's gaze fell on the Roman head. What? he thought. It's not burning. He raised his hands up in front of his face. They aren't burning either.

I'm having a vision, Fieran realized. The fire feels so real. But it isn't.

Fieran forced himself to stay still. He closed his eyes and breathed slowly. It is a vision, he repeated to himself. A vision. The fire is not really burning me.

Slowly he opened his eyes. Ready to see what the

vision had to tell him. He saw his own face reflected in the flames.

Fire had always attracted Fieran. To choose fire over water was not the way of his people. But fire called to him.

"What is it?" Fieran whispered. "Tell me."

A second face appeared, as if in answer. Now Conn's face floated next to Fieran's own in the wall of flames.

Conn's face began to grow. Growing and growing until it began to cover Fieran's face. Within moments Conn's enormous face completely covered Fieran's.

"No," Fieran muttered. "That cannot be. *I* have the power of the head. I cannot be defeated."

"Fieran!" a woman's voice called out.

"Brianna!" Fieran cried. The image of Conn's sneering face disappeared—and a vision of Brianna replaced it.

Brianna. He thought about her all the time. Whenever the people gathered he couldn't stop himself from staring at her. And when they were alone he couldn't stop himself from touching her.

In the vision, Brianna smiled at him. She stretched her arms out toward him.

Fieran reached for her.

The flames winked out. Fieran stood all alone.

I am going to beat Conn! he thought. I am going to be chosen chief—not he. And best of all, I will marry Brianna. That is what my vision means.

I will make it all happen. I *must!* Fieran swore. And that means I must learn how to use the power of the head.

Fieran knew the first thing he must do. With quick strides he crossed to the brazier in the center of his dwelling. The heavy iron basket sat on three long legs. Hot coals rested inside. Fieran took a long poker and stirred the fire until tiny flames licked over the surface of the coals.

Then he picked up the head. He shivered when he felt the cold flesh beneath his fingertips. He wanted to drop the head back on the floor.

You killed this man, Fieran reminded himself. You cannot be afraid to touch part of his lifeless body.

But killing in the heat of battle felt much different. Soldiers had to kill or be killed. There was no time to think.

Fieran stared down at the head. He felt a sharp taste hit the back of his throat, but he forced himself to keep looking. The skin hung loose. The mouth sagged open.

Strange that such a thing could hold such power. But it did.

He carried the head over to the fire and positioned it on top of the long metal rod that stuck straight up from the bottom of the kettle of coals. The rod he usually used for cooking meat.

Then he pulled down on the head, forcing the rod deep inside it. The heat from the fire will start the process, Fieran thought. He knew that the power would not be released from the head until the flesh fell away from the bones.

Fieran stripped off his bloodstained clothes and washed himself. Then he pulled on clean homespun garments and stretched out on his sleeping pallet.

He felt exhausted, but his mind kept racing. Jumping from Conn to Brianna to his father to the head.

He rolled over onto his side and watched the shadows thrown on the wall. One of the shadows appeared darker than the others. It crept across his feet and moved upward. Fieran lost all feeling in his legs.

The shadow crept across his stomach. And Fieran's stomach clenched. It felt frozen.

He tried to force himself to get up. But he felt too tired. He could barely move.

The shadow flowed across Fieran's chest. Fieran's heart began to pound in slow, painful beats.

I must do something! he thought. I cannot let it reach my head.

The shadow inched up his throat. Fieran opened his mouth to scream. No sound came out.

He couldn't breathe. He clawed at his throat, gasping and choking. The shadow is cutting off my air, he thought. I need air.

Chapter
8

"What is it, Fieran?" a voice cried out.

Fieran jerked himself upright. He pulled a shaking breath into his lungs.

"Brianna," he choked out. "I must have had a nightmare! I couldn't breathe. I couldn't move."

Brianna knelt on the floor beside him. "Hush, now, Fieran," she crooned.

"It was only a dream," Fieran muttered. He felt silly with Brianna fussing over him. But it was nice, too. Fieran breathed in her sweet scent as she ran a hand across his brow.

Brianna was the rarest of all things among the Celtic people—a female spell-caster. She also had the ability to interpret dreams and visions.

"Fieran," she said now, her voice soft and melodic. "Tell me about your dream."

Brianna took his hands between hers. She rubbed

them gently. "I can tell you are exhausted," she said. "Your hands are so cold."

"I'll warm up now that you are here," Fieran answered. Then he noticed how pale Brianna appeared. He could see deep shadows beneath her eyes. "Brianna, what is it?" he asked anxiously. "What troubles you?"

Abruptly, Brianna rose to her feet. "It is nothing, Fieran," she said.

But he noticed she could not meet his gaze.

"In fact, I come to bring you joyous news," Brianna continued. "The Romans are defeated. The day is ours."

Why won't she look at me, Fieran wondered. What is wrong?

"I knew this when I left the battlefield," he replied. The words came out sounding harsher than he intended. Before he could apologize, Brianna rushed on.

"There is more, Fieran. For taking the head of the Roman leader, you are declared a great hero." She crossed over to the brazier and stared at the grisly head.

Suddenly, Fieran remembered his vision. All his energy returned. He jumped up from his sleeping pallet. "I had vision when I returned from battle. A wall of flame appeared and . . ." His voice trailed off.

Brianna kept her eyes on the head of the Roman leader. With the head stuck on the spit, she could stare directly into the face. She appeared fascinated by it.

"Brianna?" Fieran said softly.

She shook her head and turned to face him. "What did you see?"

"I saw you," Fieran answered.

"You saw me?" she exclaimed. "Only me?"

Fieran shook his head. "No," he answered. "I also saw myself and Conn." He paused for a moment, trying to remember his exact vision.

"I saw myself first," he continued. "Then I saw Conn. He grew to monstrous size. But then you appeared, and Conn vanished."

"You saw Conn?"

"Yes," he answered. Why did she seem so distracted? "He almost overwhelmed me. His face covered mine for a moment. But I beat him. His face completely disappeared. There is only one thing it can mean. I'm sure of it."

"You think it means you are destined to become the new chief," Brianna said. Her voice was emotionless.

"Well, of course I do," Fieran said. He stared down into Brianna's face. What he saw chilled him. Her expression was solemn. Her eyes filled with tears.

Brianna is an expert in interpreting dreams and visions, he thought. What could have upset her so in his? "Tell me, Brianna," Fieran urged her. "Am I wrong?"

Brianna threw her arms around him. She buried her face against his chest. "I am not certain, Fieran."

Slowly, Fieran drew her head back. He wiped the tears from her cheeks. He kissed her tenderly.

"It is all right, Brianna. I am certain," he said. "I am certain enough for both of us."

Brianna pressed her face against his neck. "Oh, Fieran, I pray you will take care. Too often, visions only show us our own desires. We see only what we wish to see."

"Not this time," Fieran vowed, holding her closer.

"Not this time. You will see. Being the chief of our people is my fate, Brianna."

"You are wrong!" a deep voice boomed.

Fieran and Brianna sprang apart. Conn stood a few feet away from them, his arms folded across his chest. "You are never going to be chief, Fieran!"

Chapter 9

"**I** am," said Conn. "*I* am going to be the new chief."

Rage rose up in Fieran. He didn't even try to beat it down. "Never!" he cried out. "I will stop you if it takes everything I have."

"It might," Conn replied. He stepped up to Fieran, so close their chests almost touched. "It might—and that still won't be enough to stop me."

"Stop this bickering at once!" Brianna cried suddenly.

Conn stared at her with his cold blue eyes. Then he returned his gaze to Fieran. "Which of us do you think Brianna wants to win?"

"What do you want here, Conn?" she demanded, her green eyes bright with anger.

"I came to congratulate Fieran on his great victory," Conn replied innocently.

Fieran glared at Conn. A victory you wanted for

yourself, he thought. You would have happily killed me to have the head and its power.

He knew Brianna didn't want them to fight. "What do you want here, Conn?" Fieran asked quietly.

"The chief is mortally wounded," Conn said. "He has decided to hold the ceremony tonight. Tonight we will discover which of us is to be the new chief. You are summoned to the sacred glade."

It has come at last! Fieran thought. The moment I've been waiting for.

"I thought my news would interest you," Conn said. "Don't linger here with Brianna too long, Fieran. It would be a shame for you to miss the ceremony and moment when I am declared chief."

Fieran and Brianna entered the sacred glade. The trees surrounding the glade grew so close together that no sunlight ever penetrated their branches. The glade was dark and silent, even at midday.

And now it was night. Many of the people held large torches. The light flickered over the faces carved into the trunks of the trees. Faces of past chiefs.

They almost appear alive, Fieran thought. He shivered.

Someday my face will be carved here, Fieran told himself. He felt Brianna touch his arm.

"Look, Fieran," she said. She pointed to a huge wicker figure in the center of the clearing. Its torso had been lined with wooden bars to form a cage. Pieces of wood had been piled all around it.

The wicker man, Fieran thought. He did not like to think about that part of the ceremony. The part of the ceremony where the old chief would die, so that his spirit could enter the new chief.

"Fieran, look," Brianna said again. This time she pointed at someone next to the wicker man.

Conn. Conn had chosen a spot so close to the wicker figure he could have touched it.

He must be very confident that he will be chosen, to stand so close, Fieran thought.

"Wherever Conn is, you should be also," Brianna murmured.

Fieran took her by the arm and strode over to Conn. The low, eerie sound of a wooden pipe filled the air. Announcing the arrival of the chief.

Fieran's heart pumped faster as he watched the chief enter the clearing. His long robes trailed along the mossy ground.

The man held himself perfectly straight. But his steps were slow and painful. A whisper ran around the clearing. "The chief. The chief has come."

The chief paused before the wicker figure. Then he climbed inside the cage in the torso. Fieran knew what would happen next. He knew it was a great gift from the chief. He knew the chief was ill, and near death.

But a feeling of dread settled over him.

The chief planned to give up his life that night. To pass his spirit on to his successor.

"Hear me, my people," the chief called out from inside the wicker man. "Witness as I give my body to the flames."

"We witness," everyone repeated after him, their voices low.

As he spoke the words, Fieran's throat felt tight. Only the bravest of the chiefs passed their spirits on in this way. Fieran wondered if he would ever be brave enough.

"Witness," the chief went on. "Watch and wait. Wait for the sign of the one who will come after."

"We will wait," the people in the circle promised. "We will wait for the sign of the chief."

"There will be one among you who can bear the fire. One who will walk unharmed among the flames. He is the one who carries my spirit within him. He must be your new chief."

All around the clearing, the people bowed their heads. Fieran felt his blood race through his veins. *It will be me. I saw the flames in my vision.*

Fieran lifted his head. The chief gave a signal. Two men with torches stepped forward. They stopped in front of the wicker man.

The chief gazed out. His eyes moved around the clearing. They rested on Conn. They rested on Fieran.

Then the chief raised his arms above his head. The men hurled their torches at the wicker man. With a hungry roar, the dry wood flared up.

Fieran heard Brianna give a low moan deep in her throat. He grabbed her hand and held it tight.

The flames roared, higher and higher. Almost as high as the tops of the trees. Within seconds, they consumed the wicker man.

The fire scorched Fieran's face. It took all his will not to step away.

The chief gave a great shout. "I choose! I choose my successor. Let him walk through the flames!"

Fieran felt his heart explode within his chest. Power surged along his every limb.

The sensation was too intense. His knees buckled. He fell to the ground.

It has happened, he thought. *It has truly happened. I have been chosen. I am the new chief.*

He knew he had to offer proof, or the others would

never believe him. "My people," he cried, struggling to his feet. "I am chosen. Come here to me."

But his cry was drowned out by a sudden babble of voices. Through the confusion, Fieran heard Conn. "I feel the power. I am the chosen one."

No, Fieran thought. No. I felt it. I felt the chief's spirit enter me. I am chosen!

"Who is it? Who is chosen?" the people asked one another.

"It is Conn!" a high-pitched voice called out.

"No! No!" Fieran yelled. He stepped closer to the flames. "If Conn says he is chosen, then he is lying. The spirit of the chief is alive within me."

The people in the clearing fell silent. They stared at Conn and Fieran. They stood together, next to the wicker figure. Brianna stood between them.

"Proof," someone called. "We must have proof."

Fieran tried to speak. But Conn was too quick for him.

"I will offer proof," Conn declared.

Conn shot his hand out and grabbed Brianna. He pulled her from Fieran's side. "The power of the chief is strong within me," Conn shouted. "So strong that I can shield another from the fire."

Before Fieran could stop him, Conn turned toward the burning wicker figure. He pulled Brianna with him into the towering flames.

Chapter
10

"*B*rianna!" Fieran screamed out. *"Brianna! No!"*

With a burst of bright white flame, the wicker man exploded. Huge, fiery embers shot straight up into the air.

As sparks rained down, Fieran saw two people standing in the wreckage. Brianna and Conn.

Relief flooded through Fieran. Brianna! She is alive!

And Conn has proven himself chief, Fieran realized.

What happened? Fieran was so sure he felt the old chief's spirit enter his body. The force of it knocked him down. Left him breathless. How could Conn have proven he is the chosen one—when I know he is not?

Fieran uttered a roar of fury and anguish. He ran into the red-hot coals. "Here is *my* proof," he shouted. "Proof that Conn is a liar and a fraud."

"You see?" Conn countered. "You see how great my power is? I extend protection even to those who don't believe me." He stepped out of the ring of fire, holding Brianna close at his side.

Everyone rushed up and surrounded him. The others have accepted Conn as their leader, Fieran thought. Now they will protect him with their own lives.

It's not fair! He doesn't deserve it! Fieran rushed from the smoldering remains of the wicker figure. Straight to Brianna and Conn, pushing the others out of his way. "Brianna," he pleaded. "You are skilled in reading the signs. Tell them that they are making a mistake. Tell them about my vision of fire. Tell them the chief has chosen me!"

Brianna's lips parted. But any words she might have spoken were drowned out by the others. "Seize him," one cried out. "Seize Fieran. He has offered false proof. He has tried to destroy our holy ritual."

"Seize him!"

"Kill him!"

"Fieran must die!"

"No!" Conn called out in a loud, deep voice. Instantly, the glade fell silent.

"You must not harm him. Fieran must not die. Can't you see what has happened? Seeing his dreams of power destroyed has been too much for him. Fieran has lost his mind. We must show him mercy."

The people shook their heads in agreement and dismay. "What a terrible thing to happen. Brave Fieran has gone mad," one woman cried.

"Listen to me!" Fieran screamed out. "I am not mad! I stood in the embers of the fire. I came out unharmed. The spirit of the old chief moves within me. You have chosen the wrong man!"

"That's enough!" Conn cried in a terrible voice. "I pity you, Fieran. I know why you make these false accusations. But I cannot allow them to go on. From this day forth, you are no longer one of our people. You are no longer one of us. I banish you, Fieran. I banish you forever."

"Banished," the people echoed. "Fieran is banished. He is no longer one of us."

Chapter
11

Banished! How can I be banished?

Only today I risked my life for my people in battle. Today I had the chance to kill Conn. I did not, because I believed my people needed him alive.

I must get away from this clearing. I must get away from Conn. When I'm far away, I'll be able to think clearly. I'll be able to think of how to defeat Conn and take my rightful place.

Fieran dashed out of the clearing. Away! he thought. I have to get away.

His vision had lied. He hadn't won. He had been defeated. And now banished.

Everything had been taken from him. There was absolutely nothing left for him. My life is over! Conn is chief!

Fieran stumbled through the forest, his long ceremonial robe slowing him down. He kept running. Running from the image of Conn and Brianna standing in the embers. Running from the image of Conn being declared chief.

But no matter how far or how fast Fieran ran, the images refused to leave him. They were burned into his memory. They would last until the end of time.

Exhausted, Fieran stopped and gazed around him. With a shock, he realized where he was. The entrance of his own cave.

Home! he thought. He pushed aside the hanging vines and walked in. His cave was cool and dark inside.

Fieran felt grateful for the darkness. He could hide here, away from everyone. He could try to forget about Conn.

The Roman head still sat upon its spit. The orange coals in the brazier reflected off its eyes. Fieran moved toward it, staring into those glowing eyes.

"I've been waiting for you, Fieran."

Fieran choked back a cry of terror. *The head spoke!* he thought.

Then he heard a laugh behind him. He whirled around. At the entrance to his cave a figure waited. Even in the dim light, Fieran could see the hatred in its eyes.

"Conn," he rasped out, his pulse still thundering. "What do you want here? Did you come to gloat?"

"That is no way to speak to your chief, Fieran. Especially after I treated you so mercifully. You should thank me."

"You are not the true chief!" Fieran shouted. "You might be able to fool the others," Fieran continued, his voice tight. "But you cannot fool me, Conn. I'm going to find out what kind of trick you used. And when I do, *you* will be banished. Or killed."

"But I *want* you to find out how I did it, Fieran."

Fieran caught his breath. He could hardly believe his ears. Why would Conn reveal the fact that he was guilty? This had to be some kind of trap. "Why?" he demanded.

Conn moved forward a few paces. The orange light of the fire flickered in his eyes.

"I want you to know exactly how much you've lost."

"I know how much I've lost," Fieran said bitterly.

"Oh, no, Fieran. I don't think you know at all. I had to have help to pull off my little trick. I couldn't do it alone."

Fieran's whole body began to tingle. "Someone helped you?" he exclaimed. "Who was it? *Tell me who!*"

A satisfied smile flickered across Conn's face. "Brianna."

The walls of the cave closed in around Fieran. He couldn't get any air. "It's not true," he gasped. "I don't believe you."

"Oh, but I'm afraid it is true, Fieran."

"Brianna loves me. She would never betray me."

Conn gave a bark of laughter. The cave echoed with the harsh sound. "Brianna loves power, Fieran. Nothing or no one else. She will do anything to get it. Even if it means betraying you."

Fieran shook his head from side to side, as if he could drive Conn's ugly words from his head. "I don't believe you," he said again. "It isn't true."

"How else do you think I survived the fire?" Conn pressed him. He stared at Fieran with his cold blue eyes. Staring as if he could see right into Fieran's mind.

Look away, Fieran ordered himself.

But he couldn't. Conn's words held him in place.

"Think, Fieran!" Conn continued softly. "My spells are not strong enough to protect me from fire. But Brianna's are. Hers were strong enough to protect us both."

"No!" Fieran screamed. Brianna would never do that to him. They loved each other.

Conn went on and on. "I suppose I have you to thank for my victory, Fieran. You taught Brianna her first fire spells. She might not have decided to work with fire if not for you."

I can't stand any more, Fieran thought. I have to make him stop. I have to make him stop.

Fieran lunged at Conn with a high, shrill shriek of anger. He wanted to feel his hands on Conn's throat. He wanted to hear Conn's neck crack. Hear Conn squeal in pain. He wanted to put a stop to Conn's hateful, ugly words.

But he was exhausted. And Conn was too quick. He sidestepped Fieran and knocked him to the ground.

Blood from a cut on his forehead trickled down into his eyes. This is what Conn wanted, Fieran realized. This is why he lied to me about Brianna. He wanted me to attack him, so he would have an excuse to kill me.

Fieran could only see Conn's knee as Conn knelt beside him. Conn grasped Fieran by the hair. He pulled Fieran's head back until Fieran thought his neck would snap. Forcing Fieran to meet his gaze.

I won on the battlefield, Fieran thought. But I won't win this time. This time, Conn really will kill me.

"You could be a dead man, Fieran," Conn murmured in a chilling voice. "You know that, don't you? I could kill you now and no one would blame me. They all know you are insane with jealousy."

Conn released Fieran's head so suddenly Fieran

had no time to brace himself. His face smashed into the ground. His ears rang with pain. But he could still hear Conn's voice.

"I don't want you to die, Fieran," Conn said. "I want you to stay alive. And every day of your life, I want you to remember all the things I've taken from you. I want you to remember that I have all the things you wanted."

Fieran struggled to rise to his feet. Conn dug his fist into Fieran's back and held him down.

"Think about it, Fieran." Conn's relentless voice filled Fieran's head. "Think about me kissing Brianna. Think about the fact that I am the new chief. Then think how powerless you are. There's nothing you can do to stop me. After all these years, I've finally won."

Through the haze of his agony, Fieran heard Conn's retreating footsteps. He heard the rustle of vines that meant that Conn had left him all alone.

Slowly, painfully, Fieran sat up. On his hands and knees, he crawled across the cave floor. His whole body ached with bruises. Blood from the cuts on his face dripped into his eyes, blurring his vision.

I'm not beaten yet, Fieran vowed with every painful motion. I'm going to fight back. I'm not beaten until the day I die.

But before he could fight back, he must have power. Power that could come from only one place. Conn hadn't taken absolutely everything from him.

Fieran still had the Roman head.

He fixed his eyes upon the head and dragged himself toward the brazier. He never glanced away from it. He repeated his new vow with every painful inch he crawled across the floor.

You are going to be sorry, Conn.

When he reached the brazier, he used it to haul himself to his feet.

Give me your power, Fieran thought. I want your power. Power to defeat my enemies. Power to make me strong.

But the power of the head would not be released until the bones were bare.

Fieran pulled out the small knife he wore strapped around his waist. He sliced into the flesh beneath the head's eye sockets. He gagged as the sickly sweet smell of rotting flesh filled his nostrils. He turned his face away.

But I cannot stop, he thought. Not if I want the power.

Fieran peeled the flesh away from the head and tossed it into the flames.

The stench of burning flesh rose up from the brazier. Fieran coughed and choked. But he didn't stop working.

Rip! Fieran tore the right ear off with his fingers. Then he tore off the left. He tossed them both into the center of the brazier.

He seized the Roman head by the hair. He pulled the hair out in great clumps. Vomit rose in the back of his throat. Fieran swallowed it down.

He dug his fingers into the eye sockets and pulled the eyeballs out. He dropped them in the fire.

I will not stop! Fieran thought. I cannot. I will not stop until this head is nothing more than clean, white bone.

Then I will have the power I long for. I will have the power to take my revenge!

Chapter
12

The head began to pulse under Fieran's fingers. The empty eye sockets began to glow blood red.

A tremor ran through Fieran's body. The power of the head terrified him.

Did tearing the flesh away release the power too quickly? Is it out of my control? Should I stop?

No! I have lost everything already. All I have left is the power of revenge.

Putrid black smoke oozed from the skull's nose holes. Fieran put an arm across his mouth, gasping and coughing. The smoke stung his eyes so badly that it hurt to keep them open. The smell was worse than the odor of corpses on a battlefield.

The power is so strong. It has not been a day since the Roman leader died, Fieran thought. I started the process too soon.

Will I be able to use the power? Or is it stronger than I am? Will it use me?

Too late to stop, Fieran thought. He stabbed his fingers deep into the head. A searing pain shot through Fieran's body. He was on fire. He was cold as ice. All at once.

Fieran shivered. Then he began to shake. He stared down at himself. He saw his arms jerking and twisting.

His teeth began to chatter. Fieran clenched them and felt them cut into his tongue. The taste of blood filled his mouth. He spat the tip of his tongue into the brazier.

The head's eye sockets glowed with green fire. He felt them burn into his own. Then the head's ghastly mouth opened. Smoke belched forth into the room.

Fieran doubled over. His whole body heaved.

It is too much, he thought. *I've released the head's power too soon! It is too strong! It is killing me!*

Fieran's eyelids fluttered. His head spun. Blackness surrounded him.

PART TWO

Despair

Chapter
13

The New World
Massachusetts Bay Colony,
1679

Christina heard another shrill scream.

She shoved herself to her feet—and saw a huge horse galloping toward her. Before she could move, the boy in the saddle reached down and pulled her up in front of him.

What if he knows who I am? she thought. What if he takes me back to my aunt? She will kill me. I know she will.

The boy wrapped her in his thick, black cloak. The whole world went black around her. Thick, stifling black.

"Please," Christina gasped. "I can't get any air. Please let me go."

Christina felt a sudden shift in the horse's gait. We're in the forest now, she realized.

"Whoa!" the boy cried. The horse gave a high-pitched whinny.

Christina managed to shove the cloak off her face. She stared up at the boy.

"I'm sorry if I startled you," he said. "But I wanted to get you out of the storm. The trees give us some protection."

Christina opened her mouth to answer, but no sound came out. So much had happened to her today. She couldn't take it all in.

"I'd best get you to shelter," he said. "You look worn to the bone."

Worn to the bone, Christina thought, as she felt the horse move beneath her. A good description. Never had she felt so tired before. Her father's funeral seemed as if it had happened weeks and weeks ago. But it was just that morning.

"I saw lights," she managed to get out. "The lights of a farm."

The young man holding her nodded. "That you did," he said. "I'm somewhat acquainted with the family that owns the farm. That's where we're going. You'll be safe there."

The rain stopped as suddenly as it had begun, but the air remained cold. The boy threw his cloak over her again. This time, he left a space for her to breathe. Christina snuggled closer to him.

Aunt Jane would disapprove, she thought. She would call it shameful to sit so close to a boy— especially a boy Christina had never met.

But it felt right. Warm and cozy.

Maybe he's my soul mate, Christina thought. Her mother used to tell her every person had a soul mate. Someone who they were meant to spend their lives with.

She wondered what this boy would think if he knew

her thoughts. He would probably laugh himself sick. Or plunk her down, turn his horse around, and gallop away.

She glanced up at him—and found the boy staring down at her. His brown eyes were warm and friendly. And she liked the way his straight brown hair fell over his forehead.

His arm tightened around her waist. "Nearly there now."

Christina sat up straight and gazed around. Then gasped. No, she thought. He can't have brought me here. Not here.

She stared up at the weathervane on top of the barn. It was shaped like a huge black cat leaping for its prey.

"Oh, no," she exclaimed. She could hear her voice quaking. "This is the Peterson farm!"

The young man stopped the horse. "Their name is Peterson," he admitted. "Why should you fear them?"

Christina bit her lip nervously. Should she reveal what the villagers said about the Petersons? Would he be offended? How well did he know them?

"Um, several girls from the village have gone to be servants at the Peterson house," Christina told him. "Not one of the girls was ever seen again. The villagers say . . . they say the Petersons used the girls for some evil purpose."

Christina's voice dropped down to a whisper. " 'Tis said the Petersons practice the dark arts."

The young man's eyebrows rose. "The dark arts?" he echoed. He sounded shocked. "I never saw any sign of that. And I stayed with them for several days."

Christina wanted to believe him. But she didn't feel sure. A few days wasn't long to keep a secret.

"My horse went lame," the young man explained. "Mistress Peterson and her daughter aided me. They gave me a place to stay. Food to eat."

He hesitated for a moment, considering. "It is true that they are very poor," he said at last. "Their life is a hard one. Perhaps it was too hard for the other girls. Perhaps they ran away. They could hardly return to the village if they had. They probably would have been sent back to the farm again."

"Perhaps it is only mean rumors," Christina suggested. The people in the village always gossiped about the wrongdoings of others. One more reason Christina disliked living there.

"Yes," he said, as he urged the horse forward. "Rumors. That must be what it is." The young man smiled at Christina. His whole face lit up when he smiled. Christina felt her heart turn over.

"There," the young man said. He pointed to a woman with a lantern near the front door. "Mistress Peterson has come outside to greet us. Nothing frightening about her, is there?"

"Why, Matthew," the woman called out, raising the lantern. "What brings you back here?"

At the sound of her voice, a cold shiver shot through Christina. She knew that voice.

Mistress Peterson is the woman I heard talking to Aunt Jane today, Christina thought.

Aunt Jane paid her to kill me!

Chapter
14

Panic surged through Christina. She managed to escape from her aunt, but it hadn't done any good. She had run straight into her enemy's arms.

She threw her leg over the side of the horse. I can still make a run for the forest, she thought.

But the young man's strong arms held her in place. She couldn't get away.

"What is it?" he said. "What's the matter?"

"Why, it's Christina Davis," Mistress Peterson cried. Every time the woman spoke, chills ran through Christina.

She watched Mistress Peterson approach the horse. When she rested her hand upon its flank, the horse shied away.

"Whoa, Thunder. Steady there. Whoa," Matthew said sharply.

Even the horse knows Mistress Peterson is evil, Christina thought. I must get away from here!

Mistress Peterson raised her lantern high. It shone on Christina's face. She lifted a hand to protect her eyes.

"So you know Christina, Matthew," Mistress Peterson commented. "I didn't realize." Her voice sounded sweet, too sweet, like sugar syrup. Christina felt her stomach roil.

"I don't really," Matthew answered simply. "I came upon her in the road and rescued her from the storm."

"A daring rescue," Mistress Peterson purred. "How fortunate. And how fortunate that you brought her here. It will save me the trouble of fetching her later."

"What do you want with me?" Christina demanded.

"You mean your aunt didn't tell you?" Mistress Peterson said, her voice growing even sweeter. "You are to work for me. This will be your home from now on."

No! Christina thought. It can't be true. That means I'll be her slave. Now I'm just like those other girls from the village. The ones who never returned.

Christina thought back to the conversation between Mistress Peterson and Aunt Jane. She remembered the soft clink of coins that meant money changing hands.

She thought Aunt Jane had paid Mistress Peterson to kill her. But Mistress Peterson had paid Aunt Jane! Her aunt had sold her as if she were a cow or a sheep.

How clever of Aunt Jane, Christina thought. She got rid of me—and earned some money at the same time.

"You come down from off that horse, now, Christina," Mistress Peterson said. Her voice sounded warm and welcoming. "Your journey has been a tiring one."

Christina wasn't fooled. She knew it was all an act for Matthew's benefit. It was exactly the way Aunt Jane talked to Christina in front of her father. She had to be on her guard.

"Come into the house," Mistress Peterson went on. "I'll get my daughter, Emily." She started toward the house, her lantern throwing wild shadows.

"You come in, also, Matthew," Mrs. Peterson called. "I'm sure Emily would hate to miss you." Then she vanished inside.

Dread filled Christina's body. I don't want to get down. I don't want to stay here, she thought. I don't want to be under Mistress Peterson's control.

But Christina knew she didn't have a choice. Her aunt sold her. She belonged to Mistress Peterson. And there wasn't a single thing that she could do about it. At least not now.

Matthew slid off the horse. He took Christina by the waist and swung her down. He didn't release her for a long moment.

"You mustn't worry," he said. He brushed a damp curl off her cheek. "Mistress Peterson will treat you fairly. Everything will be all right."

Nothing will be all right, Christina thought. How can it be?

But she didn't share her fears. She did the only thing she could. Her footsteps dragging, Christina followed Matthew into the house.

The place was dismal. A single lantern on a table near the front window gave the only light. The walls of the room were filthy. Blackened and stained with soot.

How can anyone stand it? Christina wondered. I'll die if I have to live here.

Die here. Die here. *I'm going to die here!*

6 5

The words echoed inside Christina's head. She fought to hold her panic down.

Matthew took her arm and led her to a wooden chair. "You're tired," he said. "You should sit down."

Matthew settled himself in a chair next to her. "You needn't worry," Matthew said again.

Christina stared down at her hands. He hopes if he repeats that often enough, I'll believe it, she thought. It's so sweet of him to try to reassure me.

"I know things look bad now," Matthew continued. "But I'm sure the Petersons are good people. When I was in trouble, they aided me."

Christina looked up at him. "They *bought* me," she said bitterly.

"I know it is hard," Matthew said. "But the practice is not unheard of. Many people get their start in the New World in this way. Besides, it won't last forever."

"You don't know that," Christina said.

Matthew got up and paced around the room. Christina watched him. Taking in everything about him.

He was tall, with handsome features. His clothes weren't fancy. But they were well made. And his eyes. Christina loved their rich brown shade.

"You mustn't give up," Matthew said finally, his dark eyes filled with passion. "No matter what happens. No matter what comes."

He stopped his pacing and knelt in front of her. He reached out and took her hands. "I know what it is to face impossible odds, Christina," Matthew confided softly. "But I have not lost faith in my mission. I still carry on."

"What mission do you have?" Christina asked, intrigued by his words. For a moment, she forget about her own troubles.

"I am one of two brothers," Matthew replied. He rose and sat back down beside her. But he did not release her hands.

"We have recently arrived in the New World. But no sooner did we land, than someone stole a valuable family heirloom from us. Now my brother and I are searching for it. If it takes forever, we will get it back."

"Where is your brother?" Christina asked.

Matthew sighed. "I don't really know," he said. "After the heirloom was stolen, I stayed to search the coastal towns. Benjamin went farther inland. I have no idea where he is or when I will see him again."

"How terrible for you!" Christina exclaimed. "I know what it is to be all alone in the world. I feel for you, Matthew."

Christina didn't know what to say next. Suddenly she felt shy.

Neither spoke for a long moment. Then Christina heard the voices of Mistress Peterson and her daughter.

My time with Matthew is almost over. Mistress Peterson and her daughter will appear any second.

"I cannot halt my quest, Christina," Matthew burst out, his words tumbling over one another. "I must recover my family's heirloom. I feel sure it is very near. But when I find it, I will return for you. I promise. That is, if you will wait for me."

Christina's body began to tingle. She felt her heart turn over once again.

"I know we just met," Matthew continued. "But I also know what I feel for you. It cannot be false. It is too strong. Too sudden." Tenderly, he drew her into the circle of his arms.

Christina gave a shaky laugh against his chest. "I don't even know your full name."

"My name is Matthew Fier."

Matthew Fier, Christina thought. The name of my rescuer. The name of my love.

"I cannot do anything until I find the heirloom, but then . . ." He hesitated.

"I will wait for you, Matthew," Christina said.

Matthew squeezed her tightly. Christina gazed up at him, her heart swelling.

He must be my soul mate, she thought. The one my mother used to speak of so long ago.

No matter what comes, I will love you, Matthew Fier, she thought. *I will love you until the day I die.*

Chapter
15

"Why, Matthew," a bright voice called out from the doorway. "What brings you back here?"

Christina and Matthew jerked apart. A young woman about Christina's age came into the room. Her long, blond hair framed her face. Her bright blue eyes sparkled. She is the most beautiful girl I've ever seen, Christina thought.

And all her attention is focused on Matthew Fier.

Matthew rose, as was proper when a woman entered a room. "Good evening to you, Miss Peterson," he said.

Emily gave a trill of laughter. "How formal you are tonight, Matthew," she said. She glided up to him, and laid a hand on his arm. "You weren't so standoffish the last time you visited us."

Christina felt her heartbeat falter. Matthew's face turned a dull red.

"And you've brought our servant to us," Emily went on, her blue eyes taking in and then dismissing Christina.

I can never compare with her. What must Matthew be thinking now that he sees us side by side? Christina wondered.

"My mother will be coming in a moment to give you some instructions," Emily said to Christina. "You may wait here until then. But move over there, so you do not disturb us."

Tears stinging the back of her eyelids, Christina rose and walked to the far side of the room. She has no right to treat me like this! she thought. But she knew she was wrong. Emily Peterson could treat her however she liked. Christina was nothing but a slave in the Peterson house.

"Now, Matthew," Emily said, as she urged him back onto his chair. "You must tell me all about your travels. What have you been doing since you last left us?"

With a rustle of skirts, Emily sat down next to Matthew—leaning so close her body brushed against his arm.

Christina stared at the two of them, so close together. Get away from him, she thought. He wants me. He doesn't want you.

"Christina!" Mistress Peterson called loudly. "Come this way. I will show you to your room."

Christina could feel Matthew's eyes upon her as she followed Mistress Peterson. But she didn't dare return his gaze. If she did, she feared she wouldn't be able to maintain her composure. And she didn't want to give Emily Peterson the satisfaction of seeing her break down.

Mrs. Peterson led Christina up a flight of stairs. The

second floor appeared even more dismal than the first. Christina had not thought it possible.

"This is my room," Mistress Peterson said, as they passed the first door. "And this is Emily's room. You are not to go inside them unless we give you permission."

At the far end of the hall Mistress Peterson threw open a door. "This will be your room."

Reluctantly, Christina passed through the doorway. It was so low, she had to duck her head to step inside.

The room was small and narrow. It held little furniture. Only a narrow bed with a thin quilt and a basin and pitcher sat on the floor. A single candle gave the only light.

"Clean yourself," Mistress Peterson said shortly. "It offends me to see you so untidy. When you are finished, come downstairs."

She stepped back out into the passageway and slammed the door. Christina took another look around. It's not a room, Christina thought. It is a prison cell.

But this would be her only place of refuge. Until the day that Matthew Fier completed his mission. Until he came to rescue her.

A sob rose in Christina. She pressed her hands against her throat to hold it down. If I give way now, I will never recover. I'll do nothing but sit in this room and sob and sob.

I must learn to be strong. Matthew is strong—and I can be too.

Filled with new determination, Christina crossed to the basin and knelt beside it. She seized the pitcher and poured some water into the basin. Then she plunged her hands into it. The water felt icy cold.

Christina splashed the cold water on her face. Then

she dried herself with a rough towel. She unbound and then repinned her hair.

I feel better, she thought as she stood up. But I don't look fresh and beautiful. Not like Emily Peterson.

Emily Peterson laughed.

Christina spun around. She snatched up the pitcher and clutched it to her chest.

No one there. The sound came from below, she realized. Where Emily entertained Matthew.

Christina stood motionless, listening. Emily laughed again.

The sound cut through Christina. It cut straight through to her heart.

What is happening downstairs in the sitting room? she wondered. A thousand painful images crowded through her mind.

Matthew and Emily sitting together. Matthew holding Emily's hands as tightly as he'd held hers.

Christina's hands tightened on the pticher. The blue veins stood out along the back of her hands.

What if Matthew doesn't come back for me? she thought. What if he comes back for *her*?

The pitcher shattered into a dozen pieces. Christina cried out as the sharp pieces of pottery sliced into her hands. Bright red blood spurted from her cuts. So much blood.

Christina rushed to the door. But her hands were too slippery to pull the door open. Slippery with her own blood.

Christina wrapped one hand in her skirt and opened the latch on the door. She dashed down the corridor, blood dripping from her fingers. She felt dizzy and light-headed as she forced her feet to carry her down the stairs.

She burst into the sitting room, bloody hands stretched out before her. "Matthew! Help me!" she cried.

Matthew, Emily, and Mistress Peterson leapt to their feet. Matthew started forward. But Emily pushed him aside. She darted over to Christina and seized one of her bloody hands.

Christina screamed. Emily squeezed her hand, her sharp fingernails digging into Christina's bloody palm.

"Hold still!" Emily commanded, her blue eyes wild. "Hold still or you'll spoil everything."

Blood oozed from Christina's cuts. Emily cupped one of her hands, so she could catch every drop. Christina's ears began to buzz. Spots danced in front of her eyes.

Emily squeezed her hand again.

Christina gasped in pain. She's going to bleed me, she thought. She's going to bleed me dry.

"Blood," Emily panted. She stared down at the red liquid she held in her cupped hand. She raised it to her nose and took a deep sniff. "Fresh blood."

Still panting, Emily ran from the room.

Chapter
16

Christina's knees buckled. The world whirled around her. Matthew caught her before she struck the floorboards.

"Did you see her, Matthew?" Christina gasped out. "She wanted my blood. She took some of it."

"Nonsense!" Mistress Peterson cried sharply. She hurried forward to look at Christina's hands. "You misunderstood her actions, that is all. Emily was just trying to cleanse your wounds. You'll heal faster if you bleed freely."

"Christina, what happened?" Matthew asked. He helped her up into one of the chairs. His touch was gentle and comforting.

"I broke the pitcher," Christina said. Her ears still buzzed a little. Her head felt strange. She couldn't think clearly. "I didn't mean to. It just exploded in my hands."

"There now," Mistress Peterson said. "The

pitcher's not important. But we must tend to those cuts. I'll fetch some bandages." She bustled out of the room

Matthew grasped one of her hands in his. He carefully removed the slivers that still remained in her cuts. "We'll take care of you," he said.

Fresh blood welled up. At the sight of it, Christina began to shake uncontrollably. All her fears about the Petersons returned.

I'm not wrong, she thought. I know Emily Peterson wanted my blood. But why? Why would she do such a horrible thing?

Christina shivered. It has to be for some strange, unnatural ceremony! The rumors in the village must be true. Emily must practice the dark arts!

Horror gripped Christina. "Matthew, I can't stay—"

Mistress Peterson strode back in the room. She gave Christina a sharp look. She heard me, Christina thought.

"Cleanse her hands in this water, Matthew," Mistress Peterson said briskly. She set a basin down beside him along with several strips of fresh linen. "Then bandage them with these."

Matthew carefully bathed Christina's hands. The water in the basin turned a bloody rose color.

"There," Matthew said to Christina, when he had finished. "You should heal nicely now."

"Thank you, Matthew," Christina murmured. She wanted to throw herself into his arms. But Mistress Peterson stood watching them closely.

Matthew rose to his feet. "I must continue on to the village," he informed Christina and Mistress Peterson. "I have arranged for a place to stay there."

He gazed over at Christina, his eyes warm. "I will return as soon as I can."

Silently, Christina and Mistress Peterson walked Matthew to the door. They stood on the cold front porch and watched him mount his horse.

Christina squared her shoulders and straightened her spine. I'm all alone now, she thought. There is no one to protect me. I must be strong and take care of myself . . . until Matthew can return for me.

Mistress Peterson put her arm around Christina's shoulders. "Don't worry about Christina, Matthew," she called. "We will take good care of her."

"Thank you," Matthew answered. "I know you will." Then he spurred Thunder and rode away.

The second he disappeared from sight, Mistress Peterson grabbed Christina by the hair. She shook Christina's head back and forth. "You broke my pitcher, you stupid girl! Nobody breaks my things and gets away with it. It's the cellar for you tonight!"

Mistress Peterson hauled her inside. Christina struggled, twisting and turning. But she couldn't loosen Mistress Peterson's grip.

Step by step, Mistress Peterson dragged Christina to the dark cellar door. She threw the door open, and pushed Christina in. She stumbled on the narrow wooden steps.

Mrs. Peterson slammed the door shut. A chunk of dirt fell from the wall and landed near Christina.

"No!" Christina cried out, throwing herself against the door. "You can't do this! It isn't fair! I didn't mean to break it!"

Mistress Peterson slid the latch into place.

Chapter
17

The earth walls of the cellar made Christina feel as if she had been buried alive. Her breath came in shallow gasps.

Her eyes adjusted to the darkness. She noticed dozens of red spots along the floor and dotting the walls.

Eyes! Not spots—dozens of tiny red eyes!

Christina pressed her back up against the cellar door. I'm imagining things, she thought. There's nothing in here with me.

But everywhere she glanced, she could see them. Tiny pinpoints dividing up the darkness. Tiny red eyes.

She heard a rustling sound. The eyes moved forward up the stairs toward her. Something scurried over her feet. Christina kicked it away.

High-pitched squeals filled the cellar. A thousand scrabbling feet raced over her. Piercing her with their sharp claws. A cold nose pressed against her cheek. Another rooted in her hair.

Christina screamed. And screamed again. Rats! Dozens of rats.

She reached into her hair and pulled out a wriggling, warm body. She threw it down the cellar steps.

Thunk!

She tried to grab another one. The rats scattered, scurrying out of reach.

Christina sat down on the top step. She rocked back and forth with her back to the door. What if they weren't rats? If the Petersons practice black magic they could be—

Stop, she ordered herself. Things are bad enough without making up monsters. I've got to be like Matthew. I've got to be strong.

She wished Matthew was there with her. Holding her. Just the thought of him made her feel better.

Christina wrapped her arms around herself, trying to stay warm. She felt something hard pressed against her chest. The silver pendant. She had almost forgotten about it.

She tugged on the chain and pulled the pendant free. She cradled it in her hands. It felt warm to the touch.

Holding it made her feel comforted. Just as thinking of Matthew did.

"Get up, you lazy girl! I didn't pay good money for you just to have you sleep all day!"

Mistress Peterson opened the door to the cellar with a jerk. Christina tumbled backward and struck her head on the bottom cellar stair.

"Clumsy oaf," Mistress Peterson muttered. "If

you're not out in the yard in ten seconds, there will be nothing for you to eat this day."

Christina scrambled to her feet. Her head swam. But she forced her feet to carry her up the cellar stairs after Mistress Peterson.

She stuffed the silver pendant back inside her dress. She didn't want Mistress Peterson to see it—and take it away from her.

"Very good," Mistress Peterson said when Christina made her way out into the yard.

It's barely dawn, Christina realized. She felt exhausted. Her sore ankle throbbed and every muscle ached.

"You can begin your chores right away," Mistress Peterson said. "When you've done the first one to my satisfaction, you can have some food. Start by cleaning up the mess you made in your room yesterday. Hurry, now! I will not tolerate laziness. Go get a bucket of water from the well."

Footsteps dragging, Christina fetched a bucket and filled it with water. She slowly carried it to her room, careful not to spill one tiny drop. If she did, she feared Mistress Peterson would lock her into the cellar again.

Christina got down on her hands and knees, and began to scrub the floor. It took forever to get the bloodstains off.

She tried not to remember how the stains came to be there. Tried not to remember the sound of Emily Peterson's laughter or the way she smiled at Matthew Fier.

When she finished, her tiny room shone. That should satisfy even Mistress Peterson, Christina thought. Her stomach rumbled with hunger. She hefted the bucket of bloody water and started back downstairs.

She heard a rustling from Emily's room. Christina hurried past the door, not wanting to see the blond girl.

And she heard someone moan.

Christina dropped the bucket. Water splashed out onto the hallway floor. The moan came again, louder this time.

Is Emily sick? Heart pounding, Christina crept closer to Emily's door. She didn't want anything to do with Emily. But she couldn't ignore her. What if she hurt herself somehow?

Christina put her hand on the door. I can't just pretend I didn't hear anything. I've got to find out what's going on!

"Don't go in there!" a voice behind her shrieked.

Christina spun around. Emily glared at her from the top of the stairs.

Christina heard the moan again.

If Emily is out here—who is that moaning in her room?

Chapter
18

Emily rushed down the hall toward Christina. "Get away from there!" she screeched. "That's *my* room. You can never go inside. Ever."

What does she have in there? Christina wondered. Is a person locked in there? Who was moaning?

Emily shoved Christina out of the way. She pulled the door open a crack and quickly slipped through it. Christina couldn't see a thing before Emily slammed the door behind her.

The moaning stopped. Christina stood frozen in the hallway. She didn't know what to do.

What's really in there? she wondered. What is Emily Peterson doing? Heart pounding in fear, Christina remembered all the horrible rumors she'd heard in the village.

Rumors that the Petersons practiced the dark arts. That they captured people and tortured them. Is

Emily torturing someone now? Is that what she was doing in her room?

Christina remembered a conversation she once heard while doing the shopping for Aunt Jane.

"I hear they eat people alive," Mistress Tucker said.

"I hear they boil them and then eat them," Mistress Brown answered.

"And I hear," Mistress Dennison spoke up, her voice no more than a whisper, *"that they drain their victims' blood and drink it while it's still warm."*

I can't just walk away, Christina thought. Not if Emily's holding somebody prisoner in there. I have to find out what is going on.

She reached for Emily's doorlatch.

"Stay away," a voice behind the door whispered. "Christina Davis, stay away! Or I will make you very sorry."

Christina turned and picked up her bucket. Then she ran down the stairs as fast as she could. She didn't even stop to mop up the water she spilled in the hall. Mistress Peterson might not give her any breakfast. But Christina didn't care anymore.

All she cared about was getting away from Emily's room and its deadly secrets.

Mistress Peterson studied Christina from head to foot as she lugged the bucket into the kitchen. Then she nodded as if satisfied.

She likes my fear, Christina thought. She wants me to be afraid.

"You can throw that dirty water out into the yard," Mistress Peterson said. "And that room upstairs better be spotless when I check it later."

Christina nodded. "Yes, ma'am," she said as she headed out the kitchen door.

Silently, she made a vow to clean up the water she

had spilled as soon as she finished eating. When she returned to the kitchen, Mistress Peterson gave her a meager breakfast of thin gruel and cold potatoes. Then she put Christina to work again.

Work.

Work.

Work.

Christina's days slipped into a dismal pattern. She arose at first light. She worked all day. She fell into her bed exhausted each night. After what felt like moments, Mistress Peterson shook her awake. Forcing her to begin another day.

Sometimes while Christina cleaned, she allowed herself to daydream about Matthew. About the day he would come back for her.

Emily did no work at all, as far as Christina could tell. She stayed upstairs in her bedroom most of the time. Except for her trips into the woods.

Every day Emily went to the woods with a basket over her arm. When she came back, things inside the basket cried and wriggled.

Christina never had a chance to see what Emily brought home from the woods. Emily always took the basket straight upstairs to her room.

And Christina stayed away from Emily's room. She felt too frightened to go near it. But she could still hear the moans whenever she was upstairs.

Then, one day, Christina woke up before Mistress Peterson came for her. She couldn't figure out why— until she realized the moans had stopped. An unnatural silence filled the house.

Christina quickly dressed and tiptoed down the hall.

She pressed her ear to the door of Emily's room.

I know it is forbidden. But I must see what is inside.

If I can find out what she is doing, maybe I can stop it. And maybe I can find a way to escape from here.

"Christina Davis! Get down here this instant!" Mistress Peterson's voice shot up the stairs.

Christina jumped. She jerked away from Emily's bedroom. I will get my chance. Someday, she promised herself.

"There you are!" Mistress Peterson exclaimed as Christina hurried into the sitting room. "You're late. You'll get no breakfast. Start your chores right away."

Christina's stomach growled. I'm so hungry, she thought. If I eat any less, I'll die.

"Emily and I are going out this morning," Mistress Peterson informed Christina. "We are going to the village. You are going to stay here and clean the sitting room walls."

Something is happening, Christina thought. Something is wrong.

The Petersons rarely went to town. They knew they were not welcome there.

"Christina!" Mistress Peterson's sharp voice cut through Christina's thoughts. "Are you listening to me?"

"Yes, ma'am," Christina answered. "You want me to clean the sitting room walls."

Mistress Peterson gave a satisfied sniff. "That's very good, Christina. I'm pleased to see you're learning how to behave. It doesn't do to have too much pride, you know. Particularly not in your situation."

Emily giggled from the doorway.

Hot color flooded Christina's face. She could feel her cheeks begin to burn.

I'll discover your secret, Emily, she thought. You won't do so much laughing then.

"What a pity you can't come to the village with us,

Christina," Emily said. "What a shame you're only a servant and have to stay at home. But I'm sure Matthew will understand the reason you can't see him."

Matthew! Christina thought. Are they going to visit Matthew?

Emily smiled when she noticed Christina's upset expression. Her teeth were sharp and pointed, like a cat's.

Oh, Matthew, Christina thought. Don't be fooled by Emily's beauty. Remember your promise to me.

"I expect this room to be perfect by the time we return, Christina," Mistress Peterson said. She drew on her cloak. Tenderly, she wrapped Emily up against the chill spring air.

"Yes, ma'am," Christina answered once again. She followed the Petersons into the yard and drew a bucket of water from the well.

"Come along, Emily," Mistress Peterson commanded as she climbed into the wagon. "We've wasted enough time."

Emily marched past Christina with a swirl of pale blue skirts. Her golden hair glowed in the sun. Christina fought down an impulse to toss the bucket of water over Emily's head.

Mistress Peterson clicked her tongue to the horse. The wagon rumbled out of the yard. Christina returned to the sitting room. When she could no longer hear the wagon, she picked up the bucket and threw it against the sitting room wall.

The bucket burst with the force of Christina's throw. Dirty water streaked down the walls.

I hate you both! she thought. I will be so happy the day I leave this house forever!

Christina dashed up to Emily's room. Taking the steps two at a time.

She pressed her ear against the door. Complete silence.

Her hand crept toward the doorlatch.

I shouldn't do this, Christina thought. Emily told me to stay out. She warned me to stay away.

But her hand kept moving, in spite of Emily's warning. Christina swung the door open—and stuck her head inside.

Huge faces stared back at Christina. Their mouths open wide.

Christina shrieked and stumbled back into the hall. She expected the creatures to come after her. But they didn't. The house remained still and silent.

She slowly stood, then cautiously inched back to Emily's door. Still perfectly quiet. Christina peeked inside.

Mirrors! Mirrors covered all the walls—and the ceiling. I was frightened by my own reflection!

Christina stepped into Emily's room. It's like a shrine, she thought. A shrine to her incredible beauty.

The thought made Christina feel sick.

Holding her breath, Christina crept forward. Her mirror images crept with her. Halfway across the room, she saw it.

A human hand.

Christina gagged and covered her mouth. All around her, the mirror images did the same.

The hand sat on a shelf above Emily's bed. The wrist had been nailed to a block of wood. The fingers extended upward into the air. They appeared black and withered.

Merciful heavens! Christina thought. What kind of

evil is this? Her eyes ran across the shelf. A jar of spiders. A jar of rat tails. A jar of round white balls with darkened centers.

Eyeballs! Christina thought.

And then the moaning began.

Christina covered her ears to block out the horrible sound. A thousand panicked Christinas did the same in the mirrors all around her. Christina could see their eyes staring in terror. Their mouths gaping wide open.

Christina followed the moaning sound to a clay jar on the shelf. Nothing can make me look into that jar, she thought. Nothing. Not even if it will make the moaning stop.

The moaning grew louder. "Christina. *Christinaaaaaaa.*"

The thing in the jar is calling my name!

It knows my name!

Christina turned to run.

I've got to get out of here! I've got to run away and never come back. This is an evil, unnatural place.

She stumbled to the doorway. The door slammed shut in her face.

"No!" Christina gasped. Her knees felt weak. Her whole body too heavy to move.

The moaning filled her head. Jabs of pain shot out from the center of her brain. She couldn't think.

"What do you want? What do you want from me?" she screeched.

Then she caught sight of a tall, narrow bookcase. Its shelves were filled with tiny vials. Christina took a step toward it.

The moaning stopped abruptly. Christina moved closer to the bookcase and stared at the vials.

They were empty. A rust-colored sediment stained their sides. Each vial had been carefully labeled with a name.

Christina noticed a full vial behind the others—with her name neatly printed on the label.

Christina snatched the vial up. It was filled with bright red liquid. Christina knew at once what it was.

Blood, she thought. *My blood!*

Chapter
19

Christina hurled the vial to the floor.

Her blood ran out in a thin, red stream. It stained the floor of Emily's room.

No, Emily! You are not going to use my blood for your evil. And you can clean it up yourself. I'm leaving this horrible place.

Then she turned and bolted to the door.

The door would not budge. She couldn't move it at all.

I've got to get out of here! Away from this evil. If I don't, my heart will surely explode!

Heat spread over her chest. The skin growing hotter and hotter.

Christina's breath rasped inside her throat. She tugged on her bodice.

Tight! It's too tight!

Her fingers found something round and hot. Christina pulled it out.

The silver pendant.

It glittered in the dim light. The blue stones sparkled so brightly Christina could hardly bear to look at them.

Dazzled by the blue stones, Christina turned the pendant over. For the first time she realized that an inscription covered the back.

The words were in Latin. Christina could just make them out.

Dominatio per malum.

What does that mean? Christina wondered.

Her father had been a scholar. He had taught her some Latin.

Think! You know those words! Christina thought. You know what they mean!

Dominatio.

Dominatio meant power.

Malum.

Malum meant evil.

Dominatio per malum. Power through evil.

Piercing pain lanced through Christina. She felt as if she had taken a bolt of lightning straight to the head.

Fire roared all around her.

For an instant, a grinning skull appeared in the flames.

It's the pendant, she thought. I've got to put down the pendant.

But she couldn't do it. Her fingers were locked around it.

Christina swayed on her feet. The room around her went black.

PART THREE

Revenge

Chapter
20

The Old World
Britain, A.D. 50

Fieran choked on the black smoke that poured from the head of the Roman leader. He sat up, gasping and sputtering.

I did it! he thought. I released the full power of the head. *And I'm still alive!*

He staggered to his feet. The black smoke swirled around his ankles.

He stared over at the head. It still sat on its spit above the brazier. No flesh remained on it. The bones gleamed, clean and white.

But the eyes sockets.

They glowed green. An unearthly green.

What have I done? Fieran asked himself. Have I brought some evil to life? What if I do not have the strength to control it?

A voice filled Fieran's head.

Why have you summoned me?

Fieran screamed. He pressed his hands against his temples. The voice repeated the question over and over. Pain slammed through Fieran's head.

I must bear this, he thought. I must become the master of this pain. This is the first step toward achieving my power. I must be able to answer when the head speaks.

Fieran forced himself to take his hands away from his head. He lowered them to his sides. His hands clenched into fists—as if that could help him control the pain.

"Power," he said in a low voice. "I want all the power you have."

What kind of power?

"The power of revenge," Fieran answered.

The head laughed. The sound reverberated through the stone chamber. The black smoke swirled up from the floor.

Fieran cried out. Every sound the head made shot agony through him.

I will give you these things. But I must have payment.

"Anything!" Fieran cried, ignoring the pain.

Lightning flashed through the cave.

A creature that was half-man and half-bird flew through the opening. It snatched Fieran up in one of its sharp claws.

Fieran screamed in terror. How could such a creature exist?

A vision, Fieran told himself. The Roman leader has sent me a vision.

The bird-creature uttered a high, shrill scream as it flew out of the cave. It carried Fieran up into the night sky. Higher and higher until he could not see the ground.

Fieran forced himself to keep his eyes open. He must not miss one clue the vision would give him.

The cold air burned his face. His fingers grew numb.

The bird-creature closed its black wings. It fell straight down. Gaining speed with every moment.

Fieran heard himself moan low in his throat. A vision, he told himself. A vision.

The bird-creature released Fieran—and rose back into the sky.

Fieran fell through the darkness. His heart pounding in his ears was the only sound he heard.

He landed on something hard and felt warm blood trickle down the back of his head.

Fieran slowly pushed himself upright. He sat on a round slab of dull gray stone.

Smaller stones rested on top of it. Glistening blue stones.

Is this a place of good or evil? Fieran asked himself. He climbed down. The stone is an altar, he realized.

Carved in the stone were the words *Dominatio per malum.* He knew the words were in the language of the Romans, but he was unsure what they meant.

The words were stained with red. Blood, he realized. This is a place of sacrifice.

Fieran shivered. Suddenly he remembered his father warning him about the high price of power.

He turned his attention to the glittering blue stones. Before his eyes, each stone burst into a column of flame.

"Such power," Fieran whispered. He forced himself to step closer. And saw faces in the flames. Faces screaming and crying. Faces twisted in torment.

The flames grew stronger. The columns joined together. They formed a wall in front of Fieran.

He spun around.

Flames formed a circle around him. And moved closer. Tighter.

Fieran screamed as they engulfed him.

He screamed again—and realized he was back in his cave. Staring at his own fire.

Pulling in deep, ragged breaths he sank to the ground. The vision was so powerful, so real. He glanced down at himself to make sure he was unharmed.

And saw a strange object clutched in his left hand. An amulet on a silver chain.

Fieran's hand trembled as he studied the silver disc. The front had a silver bird's claw clutching glittering stones. Blue stones.

And Latin words were carved on the back. *Dominatio per malum.*

Power through evil. The deep voice of the Roman head boomed.

As long as your family lasts, so will this amulet. So will the power of your revenge.

Fieran wanted to throw the amulet on the ground and run. Run to a place where no one knew him. Where he could start a new life.

This power was evil. Pure evil. Could he use it without becoming evil himself?

Then Fieran thought of Conn. He remembered how Conn had cheated him out of becoming the chief.

I allowed Conn to live on the battlefield, Fieran thought. I will not show him mercy a second time.

"Revenge," Fieran whispered. "Revenge," he repeated, his voice stronger.

Blood. For your revenge I must have blood.

Chapter
21

A sacrifice. It asks for a sacrifice.

Blood . . . I must have blood. The Roman head's voice was deep and loud.

Can I do it? Fieran wondered.

He had killed in battle. But a sacrifice was different. To make a sacrifice he would *plan* to kill. Decide to kill.

He would not be killing to survive. He would not be killing because his friends and neighbors were in danger from the Roman troops.

Fieran hated the thought of killing off the battle-field.

But he remembered the way Conn taunted him. Laughed at him. "You will have your blood," Fieran answered.

Creeaaak. The jaws of the skull opened. Its teeth parted in a deadly smile. Then the eye sockets went dark. Blown out like two candles.

Fieran stripped off his ceremonial garments. He hesitated a moment. Then he thrust them into the coals. He watched as his long robes smoldered and burned.

His people did not believe Fieran when he told them the old chief's spirit entered his body. They now thought him insane. Or jealous. He had no place among them any longer.

Fieran washed the blood from his face and hands. He dressed himself in fresh garments. Green and brown, to blend in with the trees. He threw a cloak around his shoulders and fastened it with a heavy brooch as was the custom of the Celts.

There is only one person who deserves to be sacrificed to the head, Fieran thought. Conn.

The human sacrifice *must* be Conn!

Now, how to get him? Think! Fieran told himself. Think! He began to pace around the dark cave.

There has to be a way to get to Conn. It will be difficult. He will be well protected now that he has been declared chief.

Fieran stopped pacing a moment. He stared at the head as if it would provide inspiration.

Conn had to have a weakness. Everyone did. All Fieran needed to do was discover it. Once he had that, he could use Conn's weakness to trap him.

I can't discover Conn's weakness standing in my cave, he thought. I have to study him. Learn everything about him. Every habit. Every small detail.

I'll start with his house. Fieran always hated sharing the forest with Conn. But today he felt glad. Conn would be more difficult to protect there.

In the forest, it will be easier for me to get to you. I know the land much better than you do.

Fieran left the cave. Silent as a shadow, he moved through the trees. His green and brown garments blended in with his surroundings.

When Conn's thatched hut came into sight, Fieran hid himself in a nearby stand of trees. He had a good view of the hut's only door. He would see anyone going in or out. He would see Conn. But Conn wouldn't see him.

I'm waiting for you, Conn! Fieran thought. Soon you will understand what it means to lose everything.

Within moments, Conn came into sight. If Fieran had been a few moments later, he would have run right into him.

Fieran immediately noticed that Conn had no guards around. He left himself completely unprotected.

Fieran's heart leapt up. Now I know Conn's weakness. He believes he is invincible. He thinks no one will attack him, because he is too strong.

But I will show him that his strength is his weakness. I will use his pride to conquer him.

Fieran's muscles tensed. I could kill you, Conn. I could kill you now.

He watched as Conn opened the door to his house. Fieran crept forward.

"You can come out now," Conn called.

He knows I'm here! He knows I'm watching him. Fieran jerked back. His heart thundered. His breath came in shallow gasps.

What is Conn going to do?

A figure in a long, hooded robe stepped into the clearing. Conn doesn't know I'm here, Fieran realized. He wasn't calling me. He spoke to this other person.

Fieran relaxed. His heartbeat slowed down.

He stared at the person with Conn. He couldn't see the man's face. He wore the hood pulled down low.

Fieran heard Conn laugh. "Why are you still hiding yourself?" he asked playfully. He reached up and pushed the other person's hood back.

Brianna.

A hot, sour taste hit the back of Fieran's throat. He swallowed hard.

Not Brianna. She loved Fieran. He knew she did.

Conn pulled Brianna into his arms. He kissed her, a long, deep kiss.

Brianna wrapped her arms around his neck. Eagerly returning the embrace.

Conn lifted his head and ran his fingers down Brianna's cheek. "We did it!" Conn said. "We beat that stupid weakling Fieran. We fooled everyone. And now no one can stop us."

Brianna smiled. She stood on tiptoe and pressed a kiss on Conn's jaw. "No one can stop us," she repeated.

"It was so easy!" Conn cried. He threw back his head and roared with laughter. "I can hardly believe how easy."

"I told you it would be," Brianna replied.

"You told me," Conn admitted. "You were right. And I was wrong. I could not believe what idiots the others are. They thought you were my victim. They never considered the possibility that a woman could cast such a powerful spell.

"But you did," Conn continued. "And your spell convinced them that I was the chosen one. Now we will have everything we want."

Oh, Brianna. How could she have done that to him?

She knew he had always dreamed of being chief. She knew it meant everything to him.

She would never have known any fire spells if not for me, he thought. She had never experimented with fire before I began to teach her.

Now her power is stronger than mine. And she used it to defeat me.

Fieran watched Brianna. It made him feel sick.

"Together we are more powerful than all the others put together," she vowed. Her eyes shone as she gazed up at Fieran's lifelong enemy. "I love you, Conn. Nothing will ever come between us. I'll stand by you until the day you die."

Chapter
22

Fieran's stomach twisted. For one terrible instant, he feared he would be ill.

It's all true. All the terrible things Conn said about Brianna. All the things I didn't want to believe.

They are true. Every single one of them.

Brianna doesn't love me. She betrayed me. She helped Conn to become chief.

Fieran wanted to run away. Go somewhere where he would never have to see Brianna again. Somewhere where no one knew anything about him.

It is too painful to stay here, he thought. And without Brianna there is nothing here I want.

No, Fieran thought. No. He would not let the pain stand in the way of his revenge.

Revenge!

Brianna must share Conn's fate, Fieran thought. Her betrayal was worse than Conn's. At least Conn did not pretend that he cared for me. Brianna must die too.

Fieran imagined the expression on Brianna's face when she realized he planned to kill her. He imagined her begging and pleading with him for her life.

But I won't listen, Fieran thought. I'll never listen to Brianna again. I will make her pay for everything she's done.

He imagined his sharp knife slashing downward. Her heart's blood spraying out of her. Bright red and still warm. Exactly what the head required.

Which should he kill first? Conn or Brianna?

His oldest enemy, he decided. Conn.

I will deal with you later, Brianna, Fieran promised. I will let you live. For now. Only for now. Your turn will come.

Fieran crept from his hiding place. He made his way back home. His mind already working on the plan for his revenge.

So Conn thinks he is invincible, Fieran thought. He thinks that I am stupid and weak. He will soon see how wrong he is.

A week later, Fieran felt ready to set his plan in motion. He dressed in his most threadbare clothes. Then made his way to the Celt's hilltop village.

He had a message for Conn.

The people flocked from their homes as Fieran approached. They muttered and whispered, staring at him.

When he reached the village no one spoke to him. The crowd formed a large circle around him. They stared at Fieran in silence.

Fieran knew what they were thinking. They had all

heard that he had lost his mind. They all knew he was banished.

Once, he had been a great hero among them. Now he was in disgrace. They don't know what to say to me, Fieran thought. They don't know how to treat me.

It humiliated Fieran to appear before his people as he did. It hurt his pride.

But Fieran had no choice. He needed the people to believe he had given up. He needed them to believe Conn had broken him. He couldn't take any chances. He had to convince them.

If I don't, Conn will suspect something. I must not let him see my strength.

A ripple of movement passed through the circle. Out of the corner of his eye, Fieran spotted long robes. Good, someone summoned one of the spell-casters. Fieran's plan was working perfectly so far.

Fieran threw himself facedown in the dirt. He grabbed the hem of the spell-caster's robe. "Please," he begged. "I want to be reunited with my people. I repent for my accusations against Conn. My own pride blinded me. Now I want to acknowledge Conn as my chief."

Fieran could hear the people start to whisper. "Fieran is himself again."

"Rise up, Fieran," the man told him. "It gives me great happiness to see you are so recovered. Gladly, I will take your message to Conn, our chief."

Fieran felt exhilaration rush through him. But he had accomplished only the first part of his mission. He could not celebrate yet. He still had much to do.

He cleared his throat. "I beg of you, say this to Conn. Say I would meet him in the circle of standing stones. In the place of power our ancestors created, I will give him my vow of loyalty. It is time for the fighting between us to end."

"I will do this," the spell-caster answered. Fieran's heart beat a little faster. He saw the surprise and fear in the other man's eyes.

The circle of stones was old. Older even than the spell-casters. And it was very powerful. Powerful with a magic the spell-casters didn't understand.

Only the very brave dared enter the circle. Only those who felt very sure of their own power.

Satisfied with what he'd done, Fieran turned and walked from the village. He made sure he kept his head hanging down. He wanted to appear completely defeated.

There's no turning back now, he thought. Two of us will go into the stone circle. But only one will come out alive. When they see that it is I, the people will know they made a mistake.

They will be forced to admit I am the true chief.

Fieran strode quickly to the stone circle. He wanted to arrive there before Conn.

Like the Celt village, the circle of stones stood upon a hilltop. It could be seen for miles around. Fieran wasn't sure why his ancestors had built the circle as they had. There were those among his people who claimed their ancestors used the great stones to read the stars.

Fieran hesitated outside the circle. He felt small and insignificant as he gazed at the stones. He was mortal. But the stones would last as long as time.

The great stones were massive. Taller than the tallest man. They had been scarred by wind and weather until they seemed to have faces. Faces as fierce and proud as Fieran's own.

As he stared at the weather-beaten faces, Fieran felt a swift jolt of exhilaration shoot through him. He raised his arms over his head and turned in a circle. No longer did he feel tiny and unimportant. Now, he felt part of a great chain of being.

These are my ancestors, he thought. Their power is still strong. Today I will ask them to lend me their strength. I will ask them to help me defeat Conn.

"Hear me, spirits of my ancestors," Fieran cried out. "I do not come here to dishonor your holy place. I come here to right a great wrong. I come to take revenge upon one who has done a great evil.

"Lend me your strength, my ancestors. Smile upon my enterprise." Fieran could feel the amulet against his chest. When Conn was dead, he would bathe the amulet in Conn's blood. Only then would the amulet have its power.

The wind whistled around the hilltop. Fieran lowered his arms. He took a deep breath.

I can do no more, he thought. He felt his heartbeat speed up in anticipation. The moment I worked for is here at last. He would leave the circle in triumph. Or would not leave it at all.

Let the contest begin, he thought. I am ready for it.

Fieran stepped between the standing stones.

Instantly the wind died down.

No sound disturbed the ancient circle. Outside it, Fieran could see the grass blowing in the wind. But inside the circle, all was still. The silence so powerful it almost had a sound of its own.

Fieran's ears rang. His heart pounded. Sweat dripped down into his eyes.

It is the power that makes me feel this way, he thought. He shivered. The power of the stones.

Fieran walked around the circle. The stones cast huge shadows upon the ground. The air felt cold in the shadow of the stones. An icy cold that stole Fieran's breath away.

He turned to the nearest of the great stones. The face on the stone stared down at him. Stern and grim.

Help me, my ancestor, Fieran asked silently. Help me defeat Conn.

"Fieran! Where are you?" a voice called out. Fieran whirled around. Standing across the circle, just outside the stones, stood one lone figure.

Conn.

I knew he would come alone, Fieran thought. He is so confident. So fearless. He truly believes no one is strong enough to do him harm.

Fieran stepped out from the shadow of the stone so that Conn could see him. Conn moved forward between the stones. He crossed the circle with swift strides and stopped a few paces away from Fieran. The shadow of the great stone stretched out on the ground beside them.

"You shouldn't have come here, Fieran."

Fieran scooted a little closer to Conn. He hunched his shoulders up, as if afraid Conn would hit him. He made his voice weak and whining. "But I had to come here. I had to see you, Conn."

Conn smiled. He swaggered a little closer to Fieran. He didn't seem afraid at all. Fieran watched him out of narrowed eyes.

Oh, yes, he thought. That's right, Conn. You want to come closer. You want to prove that I am weak while you are strong. But I know your strength is your greatest weakness. I know your strength will be your downfall.

"Why have you asked me here?" Conn inquired. "Have you come to your senses at last? Have you come to beg for my forgiveness?"

Fieran felt hot blood pound through his head. He gritted his teeth to try to still his rage. I must not lose my temper, he thought. I must not let my pride stand in my way. If I do, I will be like Conn.

I am strong enough to appear weak. I am confident enough to humble myself. "I have," he answered in a soft, trembling voice. "I have come to my senses. Please, I beg you. Forgive me, Conn."

Conn's smile grew a little wider. Fieran took a few steps closer to him. He turned his palms up to show he did not have a weapon.

"I did not mean to challenge you," Fieran went on. "I did not mean to say you cheated to become chief."

"I cannot hear you, Fieran," Conn said. "You must speak up."

Fieran bit down hard on his tongue. His body quivered with the effort it took to hold himself back. With his whole being, Fieran longed to lunge at Conn. Longed to plunge his fist down Conn's throat and stop his hateful, taunting words.

But surprise is your greatest weapon, he reminded himself.

"I cannot stand it," Fieran cried out. "I cannot stand being alone anymore. Please let me join the others again. Please let me take part in the ceremonies. I will die if I don't have company. I'll do whatever you say, if only you will forgive me. Repeal my banishment, Conn."

Conn didn't reply.

"You were right," Fieran continued. Why isn't this working? he wondered. What does he want from me? "I was jealous. I could not stand the idea that you were chosen and I was not. I will confess this to everyone. If you will forgive me and let me rejoin my people."

Conn threw back his head and laughed. "Say that again, Fieran."

Fieran blinked. What game is he playing now? he wondered. "Say what again?" he asked.

"Say that again," he repeated. Patiently. As if he were speaking to an idiot. Or an animal.

"Say *all* of that again, Fieran. But say it here." Conn pointed to the ground directly in front of him. "I want to hear you say it on your knees, Fieran."

Fieran's heart pounded in hard, swift strokes. He wanted to grab Conn's head and tear it off.

Not yet, he thought. Not when I'm so close. Not until I have Conn exactly where I want him.

Slowly, Fieran lowered himself to his knees. His kneecaps ached as he pressed them against the rocky ground. "Forgive me," he whined. "Forgive me, Conn."

"When the Romans conquer Britain," Conn said. "When the last of the Celts have died. That is when I will forgive you, Fieran. You will be my enemy until the day you die."

Triumph surged through Fieran. Conn had taken the bait.

Now, he thought. I've got you where I want you!

Fieran lunged at Conn. He jerked Conn's legs out from under him.

Thunk! Conn's head hit the hard ground. He cried out, and tried to roll away. But Fieran sprang up and put his foot in the middle of Conn's chest.

"You're right, Conn," Fieran panted. "I *am* your enemy. I will be your enemy until the day *you* die. And that day is coming. Sooner than you think."

"Not yet," Conn ground out. "Not today, Fieran."

Conn grasped Fieran's leg and twisted. With a cry of pain, Fieran toppled to the ground. Conn leapt upon his back, bending one of his arms up in a terrible grip. Fieran thrashed and bucked, trying to free himself.

Fool! he told himself, as the pain poured through him. Idiot! You had him down, but you didn't finish him off. You gave in to your pride. You had to taunt him.

Fieran reared back with all his strength. Then he threw himself to one side. Pain shot like fire up his arm. But the suddenness of his movement loosened Conn's grip.

Fieran kicked out as hard as he could and knocked Conn away. He scrambled to his feet. Out of the corner of his eye, he saw Conn shove himself up. Quickly, Fieran pivoted to face him.

Conn and Fieran stared at each other. Fieran's lungs pumped with the effort to take in enough air. Blood trickled down into his eyes from a cut on his forehead. He could feel more blood oozing from the corner of his mouth. It tasted bitter and metallic on his tongue.

"You thought you were so smart, didn't you?" Conn choked out. "Pretending to be beaten. Luring me here."

"And you fell for it," Fieran came back. "You could hardly wait to make me crawl."

"You will crawl!" Conn screamed. "You aren't strong enough to stop me, Fieran. I am going to finish what I started. I am going to kill you. *Now!*"

Conn put his head down and rushed forward. Fieran started to leap out of the way. But his foot slipped. Conn barrelled right at him.

No! he thought. I can't go down. He'll kill me.

Conn ran into Fieran at full speed. His head smashed into Fieran's breastbone. Pain exploded through Fieran's chest. He fell to his back on the ground.

Conn leapt upon him. His knees dug into Fieran's arms. Fieran cried out.

Then he felt Conn's fingers wrap around his throat. "You are beaten," Conn whispered. Fieran felt Conn's hot breath upon his face. "I have beaten you, Fieran."

Conn pressed his fingers against Fieran's throat. Inch by inch, Conn squeezed his fingers closed. Fieran coughed and gagged. He tried to roll from side to side. He freed one arm. But he was so weak he could hardly use it.

His lungs ached as he tried to pull in air. It burned going down his dry and aching throat.

I must breathe, he thought. I must have air.

Conn's fingers pressed tighter. Fieran's eyes bulged. His ears filled with a high-pitched hissing sound.

This is the end, he thought. I'm going to die here.

And then the ground around him began to moan.

Chapter 23

Fieran's whole body trembled. He felt the ground around him heave and buckle.

What is happening?

Conn cried out in fear. His grip on Fieran's neck loosened slightly. Fieran clawed at his throat.

He heard the moaning sound again. It is the stones, he realized.

"It's the power!" Conn yelled. "The power of the stones."

The ancestors! Fieran thought. They have not deserted me! They have awakened the power of the stones!

With new strength, Fieran dug his fingernails into Conn's hands. Prying them away from his throat. He managed to draw in a shaky breath.

"The power of the stones is on my side, Conn," he rasped out. "You are evil. Even our ancestors are against you."

Fieran put his palm against Conn's chin and pushed back. Strength flowed through him. He pushed harder and harder. Then he heard the bones in Conn's neck begin to crack.

Conn's hands dropped away from his neck. Fieran sat up, coughing and choking.

He glanced over at Conn. He crouched inside the stone circle. His mouth hung open. Spit dribbled down his chin. He stared up at the nearest standing stone. His eyes wild.

The stone moaned and swayed.

He is absolutely terrified, Fieran realized.

"I'm being punished," Conn cried out. "I have violated the holy place. Now the power of the stones will kill me."

Fieran pushed himself to his feet and ran over to Conn.

"You *are* being punished," Fieran shouted. "I asked the stones to punish you."

Conn screamed—a high, shrill sound that sent a chill through Fieran. Fieran dragged him directly under the stone.

Conn fought Fieran like a wild thing. Fieran staggered back, away from Conn's clawing fingers.

Conn fell to his knees. He tried to crawl out of the circle. "I must get out! Away from the power of the stones," he screamed.

CRACK!

The standing stone above Conn rocked on its foundation. Conn cried out—but he stared up at the stone without moving.

The stone gave a groan that seemed to come from the bowels of the earth.

Then plunged toward Conn.

Conn gave one great shout. Then the stone hit him.

Conn's voice cut off in mid-cry.

The earth gave one last heave, and then stopped trembling.

The eerie silence of the circle descended. Fieran felt his legs begin to tremble. Then they gave way beneath him and he fell to his knees.

Fieran used his last bit of strength to crawl over to the toppled stone. He could see one of Conn's hands sticking out from beneath it. The rest of Conn's body was buried by the stone.

Conn is dead, Fieran thought. My enemy is beaten. But the power of the stones left me alive.

Fieran knew he could no longer use Conn's blood for his sacrifice. He had not killed Conn.

He pulled out his knife and hacked Conn's hand off. Then he stood on legs that still trembled and walked to the center of the circle. He placed the hand on the ground.

"Thank you, my ancestors," he called out. "Thank you for aiding me with the power of these stones."

He heard a laugh.

A hooded figure stepped out from behind the stone in front of him.

"It wasn't the power of the stones. It was me, Fieran." Brianna tossed back the hood.

"Brianna!" Fieran cried. "You . . . ?" He didn't understand. He couldn't think clearly. He felt sick and dizzy.

Brianna rushed to him. She fell down beside him on her knees.

"Oh, Fieran, I'm so glad you're all right," she cried passionately. "I was worried my power wouldn't be strong enough. I was worried that I wouldn't be in time."

Fieran struggled to concentrate. She betrayed me. I caught her with Conn. Kissing him. Laughing at me. At how they used *my* power to trick me.

What strange game is she playing now? "Are you saying you're the one who saved me?" he asked coldly. He stepped away from Brianna. She continued kneeling on the ground.

"But I know the truth about you, Brianna. Conn told me. I know that you loved him. I know that you helped him to become chief."

"I don't love Conn, Fieran," Brianna said intensely. She struggled to her feet. "I never loved him. I always loved you."

"I saw you together!" he accused.

"Fieran, I swear to you, my love, it is true," Brianna cried. "Conn surprised me at the ceremony. He pulled me into the fire with no warning."

Brianna gazed up at him pleadingly. Her eyes bright with unshed tears. "I had to cast that spell, Fieran. Don't you see that?" Brianna begged. "He left me no choice. I would have died."

She caught her breath and stepped even closer to him. "But perhaps that is what you want now. Is it, Fieran? Do you want me to die?"

Fieran could feel himself begin to weaken. He hated to see the tears glistening in Brianna's beautiful green eyes.

"What about later?" he said roughly. "Why didn't you expose him?"

Brianna bowed her head. "He threatened me, Fieran. He told me he would kill me if I didn't keep quiet. He told me—" Brianna's voice faltered and broke off.

"He told me he would kill *you*. You, Fieran. It was

bad enough that I cost you your dream. Bad enough that you could never be chief. I couldn't let him take your life, Fieran. I loved you too much. I still do."

"And so you killed Conn today to prove it?"

"Yes!" Brianna whispered passionately. "Yes, Fieran. When I heard of your message, I guessed you wanted to challenge Conn. I followed him to the stone circle. I wanted to help you. When I saw him choking you, I thought my life was over. So I made the earth tremble. I made the stone fall on Conn."

Fieran stared at her. Oh, Brianna, he thought. I want to believe you!

"But I saw the way you kissed him. The way he held you," he said softly.

"Oh, Fieran," Brianna moaned. "How this grieves me. I am so sorry you had to see that."

She reached out and stroked his cheek. He jerked his head away.

"It was all an act," she continued. "I had to do it. I had to make Conn believe I loved him. I didn't have a choice, Fieran. If Conn doubted me, he would have killed you. I had to pretend to love him. I had to keep you safe."

Could he believe her? Was she trying to protect him all along?

"Kiss me, Fieran," she whispered. "Then you will know I'm telling the truth. You will know you are the only one I could ever love."

Fieran slowly lowered his lips to hers. Brianna's lips were soft and loving. Fieran felt all his fears evaporate. Surely she couldn't kiss him like this unless she truly loved him.

"I love you, Brianna. I'm sorry I doubted you," Fieran murmured. His heart filled with a fierce joy.

They were together again. Nothing would ever separate them now.

"I want us to get married, Brianna," he said. "I want everything to be right between us."

"That would be wonderful," Brianna responded. She nestled her head against his shoulder. "I want us to be married too."

"We can go to the village," Fieran said. "I'm sure the elders will marry us at once . . . when we tell them about Conn."

"I will confess everything," Brianna promised. "I don't care if they punish me. All I want is to marry you, Fieran."

Fieran took Brianna's hand and led her from the circle of standing stones. He glanced back over his shoulder. This place will always be important to me, he thought. I defeated my lifelong enemy here. And I won back my true love.

Fieran lay upon his sleeping pallet. Brianna curled in the circle of his arms.

The elders married them that afternoon. All the village witnessed the ceremony. They wanted to throw Brianna and him a feast, but Fieran said no.

All he wanted was to be alone with Brianna. Hold her in his arms and forget all the horrible things that had happened.

He gazed down at Brianna. At his wife. She slept so peacefully. The firelight glinting off her copper-colored hair.

Fieran felt his heart swell with happiness. Conn is defeated. Brianna is mine at last.

Brianna opened her eyes and yawned. "Are you happy, beloved?" he whispered.

Brianna smiled up at him. "I am very happy, Fieran. We will be together always now. No one can part us. Together we will be stronger than all the other people."

Fear snaked through Fieran's veins. He had heard those words somewhere before.

"Brianna," he said, "I—"

But Brianna placed her fingers across his lips. "Hush now, Fieran. We are together, and we will be together always. I will stand by you until the day you die."

Ice rushed through Fieran's body. He shivered as he stared down at Brianna.

Her face appeared to glow with happiness. With love.

But Fieran knew it was an act. She didn't love him. She didn't love anyone but herself.

Fieran had heard her speak those same words to Conn. Those exact words. And she sounded just as sincere. Just as loving.

The ice in his veins began to boil. He knew what he needed to do. He knew what would take away his pain.

Revenge!

The desire for revenge pushed all other thoughts from Fieran's mind.

I will have my revenge. And now it will be twice as sweet. She has betrayed herself, and she does not even realize it!

Chapter
24

The New World
Massachusetts Bay Colony, 1679

Revenge!

Christina battled her way to wakefulness, her heart and mind filled with a single thought. Revenge.

No longer will I be a terrified victim. From now on I will take revenge on those who hurt me.

She stared at the silver pendant clutched in her hand. You put the desire for revenge into my heart, she thought. And you will help me keep it there. She slipped it over her neck and tucked it inside her dress.

Christina sprang to her feet. She stared in disgust around Emily Peterson's room. Then she strode over to the wooden bookcase. With a cry of rage, she grabbed it and rocked it from side to side.

The wood groaned and shrieked—then the bookcase slammed onto its side. The tiny vials flew everywhere. Christina stomped on them with her heavy shoes. Glass crunched beneath her feet.

The mirrors next, she decided. Christina yanked down all the mirrors she could reach, flinging them on the floor. She loved the sound they made when they shattered.

She raced over to the shelf above Emily's bed and pushed everything off with one sweep of her arm.

I will put an end to all the evil, she thought. That will be my revenge.

But it isn't just the Petersons who are evil, Christina thought. They aren't the ones who sold me.

I must do the thing I used to fear the most. I must go home. I must face Aunt Jane.

It felt strange to be outside by herself. She had grown used to spending all her time in the dark Peterson farmhouse. Working and working.

Spring has arrived, Christina realized. She spotted blossoms on the trees. But she didn't have much time to enjoy the beautiful day. She wanted to reach Aunt Jane's house as quickly as possible. Her aunt had gotten away with treating Christina badly for much, much too long.

Christina's heart began to beat faster when Aunt Jane's house came into sight. She felt the silver pendant grow warm against her chest.

Silently, she crept around to the back. Aunt Jane bustled around the yard baking pies.

Perfect! She's all alone. Christina moved closer.

Her aunt didn't notice. She had her back to Christina as she pulled a pie out of the brick oven. She cooed and clucked at it—as if it were a baby.

Christina felt a sharp, bitter taste at the back of her mouth. That's disgusting, she thought. She cares more for that pie than she does for me.

"I make the best pies in all Shadyside village," her aunt murmured.

"I thought vanity was a sin, Aunt Jane."

Aunt Jane cried out and whirled to face Christina. She almost dropped her precious pie, but caught it at the very last moment.

The red juice oozed out to stain the top crust. Strawberry, Christina thought. Always her aunt's favorite.

Aunt Jane's eyes blazed with anger. "Look what you made me do, you stupid girl," she shouted. "You almost made me ruin my beautiful pie."

Christina's heart hammered in her chest. Her tongue felt dry. Her throat felt dry. The silver pendant burned against her chest. Hot as a cinder. Hot as her rage.

Hot as her hatred.

As hot as Christina's desire for revenge.

"What are you doing here?" Aunt Jane demanded. "I just saw Mistress Peterson. She did not say anything about giving you permission to come into town."

"I gave myself permission," Christina answered.

Aunt Jane's eyes narrowed. "You'll pay for your boldness, Christina Davis," she muttered.

"We must talk, Aunt Jane. It was wrong of you to send me to work at the Petersons' farm. You seemed to care for my father. How could you do this to—"

"Wicked girl. Who are you to question my decisions?" Aunt Jane lunged at Christina. The pie slipped and tilted. The red juice bubbled and hissed.

Then the juice exploded out of the slits in the top crust. It spewed over Aunt Jane's hands. More juice than could ever have been contained within the pie.

Christina began to tremble. What is this evil?

Aunt Jane screamed in agony.

Christina wanted to rush to her aunt. Help her. But Christina's feet felt rooted to the ground.

"What is happening? What is happening?" she

cried. Her voice sounded small and weak. She tried to force herself to take a step toward Aunt Jane. Just one step. But she couldn't. She couldn't.

Christina watched in horror as the hot, red juice scalded her aunt's skin. Huge blisters rose on her hands. Then they burst. Thick white pus oozed out and dripped down onto the ground.

Her hatred of her aunt still pumped through her body. But she would never wish this on her aunt. Never. No one should endure such suffering.

The pie slipped from Aunt Jane's fingers. Steaming and hissing, it plummeted to the ground. Splashing the bubbling juice all over the front of her dress.

Christina felt the silver pendant grow hotter against her chest. It is causing this, she thought. "Stop this!" she screamed. "Stop this now!"

Aunt Jane frantically clawed at her hands. Trying to scrape off the sizzling juice. Blood poured from the open blisters.

Aunt Jane's clothes began to smoke. Christina could hardly believe it—the hot juice ate right through the cloth. Then it ate through the skin underneath.

Christina tried to squeeze her eyes shut. But she couldn't. She couldn't stop staring at her aunt.

Burning flesh fell away from her aunt's body. Christina could see sections of white bone.

The stench of rotten meat filled Christina's nostrils. She choked and coughed.

Aunt Jane twisted her head back and forth in agony. A thin trail of blood and saliva dribbled from the sides of her mouth. She held her hands out toward Christina. Skinless hands.

"Help me, Christina!" Aunt Jane cried.

Chapter 25

"**I** can't," Christina wailed. "I don't know how."

Aunt Jane shrieked—a thin, high sound. "Help me," she begged again.

"I didn't mean for this to happen." Hot tears ran down Christina's face. "Oh, Aunt Jane, I didn't mean to do this to you."

Aunt Jane staggered toward Christina. Her clothing smoked and smoldered. The steaming juice continued to burn her flesh away.

Christina's nostrils filled with the smell of burning fabric and cinnamon. Sweet strawberries and smoking flesh.

"Please," Aunt Jane gasped. "Please, Christina, I'll do anything you ask. Help me."

Christina almost couldn't bear to look at her aunt's face. It was swollen and bleeding. Her cheekbones poking through her skin.

Aunt Jane opened her mouth to scream, but no sound came out. The hot pie juice squirted into her mouth. She gurgled and choked as the searing juice ran down her throat.

Her eyes rolled back in her head. Then her legs collapsed beneath her. Aunt Jane lay still upon the ground.

Christina began to shake. Her teeth chattered together. Her knees could barely hold her up.

But she could move again. She had been released from the force that held her in place.

When Christina bolted from the yard nothing remained of Aunt Jane but a pile of smoking bone and steaming grease.

Chapter
26

Christina gagged. She raced around to the front of the house. She pulled in deep breaths of the fresh spring air.

What have I done? What have I done?

Nothing, she told herself. You have done nothing. You did not want Aunt Jane to die.

Christina hurried away from the house. Her stomach twisted inside her. There were times when she had wished for Aunt Jane's death. The day of her father's funeral she wished Aunt Jane had been the one to die.

But wishing was not the same as truly wanting her aunt dead. And no one deserved the torment her aunt had received.

Christina rounded the corner—and ran straight into Matthew.

"Christina!" Matthew cried. "What on earth are you doing here?"

"I had an errand to run in town," Christina answered. Should I tell Matthew what has happened?

She decided not to confide in him. Not yet. He could not possibly understand. She did not understand what happened herself. "What are *you* doing here?" she asked instead.

"The most wonderful thing happened!" Matthew exclaimed. Excitement shone in his dark eyes. "I felt a burst of power, just a moment ago. It could only come from the object I'm seeking. I'm sure it must be very near. I know I will find my family heirloom now."

"That's wonderful news, Matthew!" She tried to sound happy. She knew how much the heirloom meant to him. "Can you tell where the heirloom is now?"

Matthew cocked his head to one side, as if he were listening for something. "The burst of power has faded," he said. Some of the sparkle left his eyes.

"I can no longer tell where the heirloom is," Matthew continued. "But it's here, Christina," he assured her. "It's somewhere in this village. I know it is. When I find it, we can go away together."

"Oh, yes, Matthew," Christina said. She wanted to go far away, where nothing would remind her of Aunt Jane or the Petersons. Where she could start a new life.

Her aunt's death began to fade from her mind. It didn't seem quite real to her. Am I still under the influence of the pendant? she wondered.

Then Matthew pulled her to him, and Christina forgot about everything but him. She could feel his heart beating deep inside his chest. He tilted her face up and stared down at her. Then he pressed his lips to hers.

Matthew's lips felt warm and tender. Matthew, she thought, I love you with all my being. I love you until the end of time.

"It's been so hard to stay away from you, Christina," Matthew whispered in her ear. "I've thought about you every single day. But I couldn't come to the farm. I couldn't allow myself to get distracted. I have to find my family heirloom. Nothing can stand in my way."

"It is all right, Matthew," Christina assured him. "I understand."

He thought about me. Christina's face broke into a huge smile. Maybe as often as she thought about him.

But what will I do until he finds his heirloom? I can't stay at the Petersons'. Where will I live? What will I do for food?

Christina felt tears sting her eyes. She hadn't cried at the Petersons'. Not even when Mistress Peterson had locked her in the cellar. She didn't want to cry now. In front of Matthew. She pulled away from him.

"Christina! What is it?" Matthew cried.

"The Petersons are horrible, Matthew!" Christina burst out. She could no longer keep the truth to herself. "I know they were kind to you. But they have never been kind to me. Not for one instant. They are not the good people you think they are."

Matthew shook his head. "I'm sorry. I don't know what to say."

"Come back with me, Matthew," Christina begged. "Come back with me to the Peterson farm. Then you'll see what they are really like. They won't be able to hide the truth this time."

"Very well," Matthew agreed. "If the Petersons mistreat you, I can't let you stay with them. I want to search the area. Maybe I'll feel the power again. Then we can ride to the Petersons' on Thunder."

Matthew led Christina to his horse and helped her mount up. Together, they set off for the Peterson farm.

Christina could hear Emily screaming as they rode up to the farm that night.

"I went into her room," she admitted to Matthew in a low voice. "I saw the evil things she hides there . . . and I destroyed them. Now she wants to punish me for it."

"Don't worry," Matthew said. "I'm not going to leave you alone with her for one moment." He jumped off Thunder. Then he swung Christina out of the saddle and gently placed her on the ground.

Christina knew she would have to face Emily any moment. But she did not feel fearful. Matthew loved her. Their love would survive. It would triumph over Emily's evil.

Emily ran out the front door. Her cheeks flushed with anger. "Christina Davis, there you are!" she cried.

Christina stood up straight and stared Emily in the eye. "I've seen what's in your room, Emily. I know what you are. I know that you practice the dark arts."

Emily uttered a high-pitched laugh. She sounds hysterical, Christina thought.

"You stupid fool," she exclaimed. "You can't even begin to know what I am."

There's something different about her, Christina thought. Something wrong. Her face has changed. But how?

"You went into my room without permission. You destroyed my property!" she cried.

"Emily, I don't—" Matthew began.

"Stay out of this," Emily snapped, her eyes locked on Christina. "You have no idea what you are dealing with."

Emily rushed at Christina. Her hands curled into deadly claws.

Christina sidestepped quickly. She ran around Thunder so the horse stood between her and Emily.

Emily screamed and reached out to scratch Christina's face. Thunder shied and jerked his head up. Matthew grasped the bridle and tried to calm the horse.

Emily squealed in frustration. She darted forward and bit the horse on the flank.

She is insane, Christina thought.

Thunder pulled his lips back over his powerful teeth. He reared up on his hind legs. His razor-sharp front hooves flailed in the air.

Emily ducked under the horse and grabbed Christina by the hair.

Thunder bolted, pulling Matthew along with him.

Christina jerked her head back and forth, fighting to free herself. I can't let Emily take me! I can't go back inside the Peterson house. If I do, I'll never come out again.

But Emily was stronger than Christina. Inch by inch, she dragged Christina across the yard. "Noooo," Christina moaned, her voice filled with pain.

Christina turned and twisted, trying to loosen Emily's grip. Emily yanked Christina's head so hard Christina saw stars.

"Oh, no, Christina Davis," Emily muttered. "You're not going to get away from me."

Bump. Bump. Bump.

Emily pulled Christina up the front steps. She kicked open the farmhouse door and pulled Christina across the threshold. She released Christina's hair and gave her a shove that sent Christina sprawling. Christina crawled across the floor. Then she staggered to her feet and faced Emily across the dismal sitting room.

Blood dripped down from Emily Peterson's chin. It stained the front of her snowy white collar. "You stole from me," Emily shouted. "And now I am going to make you pay."

"Oh, no you're not," Christina shouted back. Her scalp throbbed where Emily pulled her hair. *"You* stole from *me!* My blood is not your property, Emily," Christina yelled. "You have no right to use it for your evil deeds."

"But I need it," Emily shrieked. "I must maintain my beauty. I must have your blood."

Christina's whole body began to tingle. I know what is different, she thought. Emily's beauty. It's fading.

Before Christina's eyes, wrinkles spread over Emily's face. Brown spots appeared on her soft white hands. Her back curved over—forcing Emily into a stoop.

Emily screeched. "Give me blood. I need your blood." Her teeth turned yellow, then black. One by one, they began to fall out.

"My beauty!" Emily sobbed, clawing at her face. "You took my beauty away."

Mistress Peterson dashed into the sitting room. She set a lighted candle down on a table. Then she took Emily into her arms.

"Now, mother," she crooned, glaring at Christina. "Don't worry. We'll get your beauty back. But first, you've got to calm down."

"Mother?" Christina gasped. "Emily is your mother?"

"Yes!" Mistress Peterson cried. "She is my mother. I would do anything for her. For years, we've been happy. People may have suspected us of practicing the dark arts. But they could never prove anything."

"My beauty," Emily wailed. "My beauty."

"I never should have brought you here," Mistress Peterson snarled. "I thought you would be another easy victim. But I was wrong."

Christina's stomach turned over. Now she knew what had happened to the other girls from the village. Emily used their blood to stay young and beautiful. She drained them dry.

"I am glad I destroyed everything in your room," Christina cried out. "You are even more evil than I thought you were."

With a cry of rage, Emily jerked away from Mistress Peterson. She leaped over to Christina and raked her nails across Christina's cheek.

Christina grabbed Emily's wrists. Her muscles trembled as she fought to keep Emily away from her.

"Destroy you. Destroy your beauty," Emily moaned. She broke free and wrapped her hands around Christina's throat.

"Matthew!" Christina cried out. "Help me." She heard Matthew's feet on the front porch.

He burst into the sitting room. He grabbed Christina by the shoulders and yanked her away from Emily.
Rriiipp!

The bodice of Christina's dress tore open. Pieces of the fabric dangling from Emily's hands.

Flash! The candlelight flashed across the silver pendant around Christina's neck.

"That is the Fier amulet!" Matthew cried. "My family's heirloom. That is what I've been searching for!"

PART FOUR

The Curse of Fear

Chapter
27

The Old World
Britain, A.D. 50

Fieran held the silver amulet up in front of him. You are beautiful, Fieran thought. And you will give me my revenge. A revenge that will last for all eternity.

Dominatio per malum. Power through evil.

If I can't have love, I will have power. I will take it any way I can.

Fieran stirred up the coals in the iron brazier. Sparks shot up into the air. Above the fire, the white skull of the Roman soldier glowed. But the eye sockets were still dark. They would not burn with their green fire until Fieran performed his deadly ceremony.

They would not burn green until Brianna's blood flowed.

Fieran moved to the sleeping pallet and stared down at her. Oh yes, you are powerful, my beautiful Brianna, he thought. But you are as false as you are lovely. And you must pay for your treachery. Your power will not save you this time.

This time, it will not be strong enough.

At last, I will have my revenge.

He slipped the amulet around his neck, and bent low over the sleeping figure of his wife. "Brianna," he called gently. "Beloved, arise!"

Brianna stirred at the sound of Fieran's voice. She opened her eyes. "Fieran, what is it?" she asked. "Is something the matter? It is not yet dawn."

She sounds so concerned. So sweet and innocent. But Fieran knew better. She would not fool him again.

"Nothing is wrong," Fieran assured her. He kept his voice low and soothing. "But there is something that we must do. We must perform a special ceremony, beloved. Now, before the rising of the sun."

"What ceremony?" Brianna asked.

"The ceremony of complete power," Fieran answered. Brianna sat up quickly.

"You would share the power of the head with me?" she exclaimed.

Fieran almost laughed at her eagerness.

Oh, Brianna, he thought. Your desire for power is so strong. If only you desired me even half so much. We might have been happy.

"Of course I wish to share the power of the head with you, Brianna," he answered. "You are my wife. I wish to share everything with you."

"Oh, Fieran!" Brianna threw her arms around his neck. Fieran could feel her heart racing.

"Come," he said. "We must begin the ceremony. It is almost dawn."

Together, Fieran and Brianna crossed to the brazier. Fieran threw a handful of peat upon the coals.

Instantly, the flames leapt up. They surrounded the Roman head. It sat grinning upon its spit.

Fieran took the amulet from around his neck. He hung it around the Roman head. It dangled down toward the flames. The silver shimmered in the fire-light.

At the sight of the amulet, Fieran heard Brianna catch her breath.

You want that, don't you, Brianna? That is very good. Keep on wanting it, Brianna. Let your desire cloud your judgment.

From the belt of his tunic, Fieran took out a black-handled knife. He chanted over it. Then he thrust the blade into the flames.

A low moaning filled the cavern. The eye sockets of the Roman head gave off the faintest green glow.

Now Fieran took up a silver goblet. He poured three drops of water into the flames. Each place the water touched, tiny blue flames sprouted up. The blue stones in the amulet blazed.

Next Fieran took out a long, black feather. When she saw it, Brianna gave a low moan. It was a feather from a crow, the bird of bad omen. Just looking at it could bring bad luck.

"Are you afraid, Brianna?" Fieran asked. "Do you want me to stop?"

Brianna's green eyes were wide. She stared at him as if she had never seen him before.

"I am not afraid," she answered. But he heard her voice tremble a little. "Continue with the ceremony, Fieran."

The blood pounded in Fieran's head as he pushed the crow's feather into the center of the fire. *So close. I am so very close now.*

The sharp scent of scorched feather filled the cave

and stung Fieran's nostrils. He held his breath and blinked his eyes. A column of black smoke curled up from the feather. Around it danced the three blue flames.

With his right hand, Fieran reached out and retrieved the knife. He held his left hand above the brazier, palm open. He took a deep breath.

My hand must be steady. I must not let my courage fail me. Not now.

Fieran breathed out quickly through his nose. He brought the knife blade down in one swift stroke. The hot tip of the knife slashed across his palm.

Pain shot up Fieran's arm. Blood from the cut dripped down into the fire. The eye sockets of the Roman head blazed a little brighter. Fieran clenched his fist, squeezing out as much blood as possible. Then he turned to Brianna.

"Your turn now, Brianna," Fieran told her.

Brianna stepped up to the brazier. Slowly, she raised her palm. She held it over the fire, just as Fieran had done before her.

Fieran's heart beat so hard his whole arm trembled.

Now! his heartbeats urged. *Do it now! Rid yourself of this traitor. Take your revenge.*

He lifted the blade above Brianna's palm. Then brought it down. But he didn't aim it at her palm.

He brought it straight down at Brianna's unprotected heart.

Chapter
28

"Traitor!" Fieran screamed. The blade plunged toward Brianna. "You lied and betrayed me. For that, you must die."

Brianna raised her arm at the very last second, blocking his. *Crack!* Their wrist bones smashed together. The knife stopped inches from Brianna's chest.

"No, Fieran," Brianna said. "Conn was right. You are stupid and weak. And it is you who are going to die."

Fieran howled in outrage. With all his strength, he tried to force the knife point down. But Brianna's arm held steady. Her brilliant green eyes locked onto his.

Look away! Fieran thought. She can cast a spell with a look. Don't stare into her eyes!

Too late. Fieran could feel the muscles in his arms begin to tremble. Then his whole body shook. A great weariness came over him. He wanted to lie down and sleep. That's all he wanted. Sleep.

Using his last ounce of strength, Fieran tore his gaze away from Brianna's. "No!" he panted. "I won't allow you to do this to me, Brianna. *No!*"

Brianna laughed. "You are as weak as a baby. You will never be able to kill me, Fieran. I am too strong for you. I always have been. I always will be. You underestimated me—as all the others did."

With one sudden motion, Brianna jerked her arm up. Fieran's grip on the knife weakened. Brianna swept it from his hand.

She brought the hilt down upon his head. Fieran sank to his knees, black dots exploding in front of his eyes.

"It would have been better if you had not challenged me, Fieran," Brianna said.

Fieran gazed up at her. *This is the end of everything.*

Brianna plunged the knife into his chest.

Fieran's blood exploded from his body.

He saw it spurt out in a great arc.

His hot blood sprayed across his face, his chest, his legs.

Too much blood, he thought. Too much blood.

He pressed his hands over the hole in his chest. But the blood ran out through his fingers.

Brianna, you have killed me, Fieran thought.

Fieran struggled to stand. I want to see the forest, he thought. Just one last time.

But his legs refused to obey him. He shoved himself to his knees, then tumbled over onto his side. He lay still. Panting and gasping.

Fieran watched his blood spread out like a lake on the floor.

"Watch me, Fieran," Brianna called. She reached

up for the silver amulet. It twisted on its long chain. The blue stones turned red in the glow of the fire.

"You thought I wanted you," Brianna said. "Just as Conn thought I wanted him. But both of you were wrong, Fieran. You were both blind fools."

Fieran felt the life draining out of him. Flowing out of him with his blood.

"There is only I one thing I want. Only one thing I have ever wanted."

"Power," Fieran rasped out.

Brianna nodded. "Power is the only thing worth wanting, Fieran."

Fieran's chest felt tight. His breath came in and out in ragged gasps.

But he no longer felt any pain. A soothing numbness filled his limbs.

I will die very soon now, he thought. And Brianna will have all the power she wants. She will have the amulet.

The amulet!

Fieran watched as Brianna knelt down beside him. She held the amulet in her right hand. She pressed the disc of silver against Fieran's chest. Fieran's heart's blood flowed over it.

She uses my blood to bring power to the amulet. She made me *her* sacrifice.

Brianna stood up swiftly and held the amulet out toward the Roman head.

"Blood!" she cried in a loud voice.

The eye sockets of the Roman head glowed. Blazing so bright, so bright green, that Fieran winced.

Revenge, he heard the head say in its ghastly voice.

Fieran's eyes flew open. I see now, he thought. Too late, I understand.

He gave a terrible laugh. Blood bubbled up into his

throat. Fieran choked and coughed. "Revenge," he gasped out, staring up at the head of the Roman leader. The powerful warrior he killed.

Father, you were right, Fieran thought. I am paying for my bargain after all.

"Your revenge," he said to the Roman head. *"Your* revenge, not mine. Your revenge on me for killing you."

The head opened its jaws and laughed. The sound echoed off the walls of Fieran's cave.

Revenge, the head boomed again. *Your blood. My revenge.*

"And mine," Brianna said. "My revenge, for all the years of being thought weak and helpless." Brianna thrust the bloody amulet into the fire. Then she pulled it back, still smoking with heat, and hung it around her neck.

The eyes of the Roman head began to pulse. Brianna threw her arms above her head.

"Power," she cried out. "I can feel the power, Fieran. Power to last for all eternity."

Brianna knelt down on the floor beside him. She took his head between her hands.

"I'm sorry that you have to die like this, Fieran."

"Save your sorrow," he gasped out. "It will not last long. Neither will your power."

Brianna's grip on his head tightened. In some far corner of his mind, Fieran knew that it should hurt. But he felt nothing now.

"What do you mean?" Brianna demanded.

Fieran drew a deep breath. Bloody bubbles foamed between his lips. "The power will not last for all eternity," he said. "Just for your lifetime. The power will die with you."

"No!" Brianna cried out. "The power of the amulet is supposed to last forever."

"As long as my family lives," Fieran said. "But we have no children, Brianna. You killed me before we could create any. So now the power of the amulet will die with you."

He stared up at Brianna. He wanted the horror on her face to be the last thing he saw.

But Brianna's expression changed from fear to triumph. "I would not be so sure of that, Fieran."

Fieran struggled to take in a breath. "What are you saying?" he demanded.

"I am saying that I carry your child."

His child! Fieran could hardly believe it. They had only been married for one night.

"You can't know that," he gasped out. "It's too soon. You can't know."

"I am absolutely certain, Fieran."

At the horrified expression on his face, Brianna laughed. "Do you think I am powerful enough to kill a man, but cannot read the changes in my own body? My power tells me I am pregnant. It tells me everything I need to know."

Brianna rose and crossed to the brazier. Above her shoulder, the eye sockets of the Roman head glowed.

She can't be certain, Fieran thought, as he stared at her. It can't be true.

But he remembered how powerful Brianna was, even without the amulet. And in his heart, he knew her words were true.

"The child will be a boy, Fieran," Brianna went on. "He will never know you. But I will make sure you are not forgotten. I will name him after you. His name and his power will live for all time."

"Brianna," Fieran pleaded. "Brianna, no."

"I will call our boy-child *Fier,* Fieran. He will be the first in a line that will continue hundreds and hundreds of years."

"Don't do this, Brianna. I beg you," Fieran choked out.

Brianna shook her head. "It is too late for regrets, Fieran. Our family, *your* family, will live forever. And so will the power you helped me create."

Dominatio per malum. Power through evil.

A curse, Fieran thought. I brought a horrible curse on my family. And the amulet is the sign. The sign of the evil I released into the world.

Into my own family.

I cannot stop it, he thought. But I am sorry.

Sorry that I brought the silver amulet into this world.

The sign of fear.

Chapter
29

The New World
Massachusetts Bay Colony,
1679

"The Fier amulet!" Matthew cried out. "My family heirloom. You had it all the time!"

"Matthew!" Christina exclaimed, horrified by his strange expression. "You must believe me. I didn't know."

Matthew started toward Christina. But Emily jabbed him in the stomach with her elbow and shoved him away.

"Beautiful. Beautiful. It must be mine!" Emily dove for Christina. Her withered hands reached for the silver amulet.

The amulet grew warm around Christina's throat. No, she thought. Oh, no. It is happening again!

"Run!" Christina screeched. But it was too late.

She tried to tear off the amulet. But she could not move.

The candle on the table exploded. Sparks showered across the floor. The dry wood floor.

Fire raced along the floorboards. Flames leaping higher and higher. Consuming the walls and the ceiling.

The fire raced like lightning up Emily's dress. Emily screamed. She reached down to tear the burning fabric from her body. The fire leapt onto her hands.

It raced along her arms. Up her shoulders. Up her neck.

Emily whipped her head from side to side. The edges of her long blond hair touched the fire—and her whole head burst into flames.

Hunks of burning hair flew toward Christina. The hot embers scorched her.

"Mother! Mother, no!" Mistress Peterson screeched. She flung herself on Emily, trying to smother the fire with her body.

But the fire burned too hot. Mistress Peterson's thick skirts went up like a torch.

"Mother!" she cried out once more.

And then Christina heard nothing but the roar of the flames.

They are dead. They are both dead!

Suddenly Christina could move again.

"Matthew!" Christina screamed. "Help me!" She could not see him. The smoke in the room was too thick.

"I'm here," Matthew called out. But Christina still could not see him.

A wall of fire cut the room in half. She stood on one side. Matthew on the other. "Matthew!" Christina cried again.

Craaack!

The ceiling above Christina split open wide. One of the support beams crashed down. Pinning Christina beneath it.

"Matthew, where are you?" Christina shouted.

Matthew burst through the fire. His wore his coat wrapped around his head to protect him from the flames.

"Over here!" Christina shouted. "I'm trapped."

Matthew dashed to her side.

"Matthew! Thank goodness!" Christina exclaimed. "The flames are everywhere and I can't move."

Matthew reached down.

Christina reached up.

Matthew grabbed the silver amulet. He tore it from around Christina's neck.

"This is my family's heirloom! You had it all the time!"

He only cares about the amulet, Christina thought in sudden terror. He doesn't care about me at all.

"Matthew," Christina said. "You must believe me. I didn't know. I never would have kept the pendant for myself if I had known it belonged to you. I would give anything to you, Matthew. I love you."

Matthew cradled the silver amulet between his hands. Then he stared down at Christina, a dazed expression in his eyes.

"Love," he repeated. "I thought I loved you. I truly did. But I know the truth now. I felt the call of the amulet—not love."

Matthew shook his head. "I don't love you. I've never loved you at all."

He's going to leave me, Christina realized. He's going to leave me here.

"Matthew!" she cried. "Don't do this! No! Don't let me die here."

Matthew put the amulet around his neck. Then he turned toward the door.

"Matthew," Christina called again. But her voice

was drowned out by the groan of the ceiling above her head.

Sparks rained down from the ceiling like shooting stars. Flames licked at the remaining beams.

But Matthew paid no attention. He strode through the wall of flames. "I have the amulet!" he cried out, his voice joyful. "The Fier amulet is mine!"

Chapter
30

Christina gasped and choked. Smoke filled the room.

She needed air. She needed fresh air to breathe. To stay alive.

A piece of burning wood hurtled toward her from the ceiling. Christina tried to roll away from it. Tried to keep the fire away from her hair. But her legs were still trapped beneath the beam.

Bang! The chunk of wood slammed into the floor inches above Christina's head.

I'm not going to let this happen! she thought. I'm not going to die here!

Christina thrust her legs against the beam. The smoldering wood groaned. She felt it give—just a little.

Pain shot up her legs. *My legs! What if they're broken?*

Don't think about that, Christina told herself. Concentrate on moving this beam. Concentrate on getting out of here.

Christina struggled to sit upright. Then she grabbed the beam with both hands. She gasped as the hot wood burned her palms. She pushed it as hard as she could. Every muscle working.

The beam rolled once. Then it rolled again.

Christina yanked her legs out from under it.

I did it! I'm free!

Christina scrambled to her hands and knees. She screamed as the blood rushed back into her legs. But she staggered to her feet.

The fire roared all around her now. I'm completely surrounded, she thought. Christina pulled off her petticoat. She wrapped it around her head.

And then she ran. Ran with all the strength she still had left within her. Ran through the towering flames.

The flames beat against Christina's face. Even through her petticoat, she could feel the fire singe her hair.

Sweat poured down her face. It stung her scorched skin.

Christina burst through the wall of flames. She heard the ceiling cave in behind her.

She yanked the Petersons' front door open. Her petticoat burned like a fireball. She whipped it off and dashed into the yard.

Matthew Fier galloped past her on Thunder.

He never looked back.

Christina sank to her knees in the Petersons' front yard. Oh, Matthew, Christina thought. You were right. I see that now. You loved your family's heirloom. You wanted it more than anything else.

But you never wanted me. You never loved me!

That disc is the sign of the life Matthew has chosen, she thought. The sign of what Matthew will become. She shivered, in spite of the heat of the fire behind her.

Christina remembered the words engraved on the back of the amulet.

Dominatio per malum. Power through evil.

Those words are a curse, she thought.

Oh, Matthew, what have you done? Now you will never know happiness. Now you will never know love.

You have traded your soul for power—and a lifetime of evil.

I loved you, Matthew. We could have made a life together.

But you chose a different way.

You chose the sign of fear.

About the Author

"Where do you get your ideas?"

That's the question that R. L. Stine is asked most often. "I don't know where my ideas come from," he says. "But I do know that I have a lot more scary stories in my mind that I can't wait to write."

So far, he has written nearly five dozen mysteries and thrillers for young people, all of them bestsellers.

Bob grew up in Columbus, Ohio. Today he lives in an apartment near Central Park in New York City with his wife, Jane, and son, Matt.

The Fear family has many secrets.
The family curse has touched many lives.
Discover the truth about them all in the

FEAR STREET SAGAS

Next . . .
THE HIDDEN EVIL
(Coming mid-January 1997)

Timothy Fier has a story to tell. A story so
frightening only a Fier could tell it. It is the story
of an evil little boy. A boy who kills.

Are you ready to hear Timothy's story?